the PaLOMiNO ☆ PONY RIDES OUT

Look out for:

the
PALOMINO
☆PONY
COMES
HOME

the
PALOMINO
☆PONY
WINS
THROUGH

the PALOMINO ☆ PONY RIDES OUT

OLIVIA TUFFIN

nosy crow

With special thanks to Michelle Misra

First published 2014 by Nosy Crow Ltd
The Crow's Nest, 10a Lant Street
London SE1 1QR
www.nosycrow.com

ISBN: 978 0 85763 308 8

Nosy Crow and associated logos are trademarks
and/or registered trademarks of Nosy Crow Ltd

A CIP catalogue record for this book is available from the British Library.

Printed and bound in the UK by Clays Ltd, St Ives Plc.
Typeset by Tiger Media Ltd, Bishops Stortford, Hertfordshire

Papers used by Nosy Crow are made from wood grown in
sustainable forests.

3 5 7 9 8 6 4

www.nosycrow.com

For my Lara,
such a special summer
O.T.

PROLOGUE

"Are you listening, Alexia?"

The voice echoing around the yard broke into the girl's thoughts. She stared blankly at her new home: Seven Birches. An Olympic-sized arena lay just in front of her and, behind that, fields stretched as far as the eye could see. There was even a horse walker to ensure the horses could be exercised in all weather. The yard had been kitted out with the best that money could buy and Alexia should have been excited about living there, but she just wasn't. She opened her mouth to speak but before she even had a chance to reply, her stepfather's voice had cut in again.

"I said, are you listening, Alexia?"

"Yes, Joe," she answered meekly.

Alexia knew that her stepfather had stretched himself to the limit to buy this place and was walking a tightrope to keep his head above water, but did he really need to be so on edge and snappy? Sighing, she wondered what was preoccupying him this time. How to make his next million, no doubt. Money and horses were his absolute obsessions. He had been a famous showjumper in his youth and he was determined that she should follow in his footsteps.

But how can I? Alexia thought to herself. *I'm absolutely terrified of jumping and I don't even care*

about winning competitions.

Alexia thought of the one thing in her life that she did really care about – her pony, River. She longed just to be able to ride him bareback with nothing more than a halter, but Joe would never allow that. Joe liked hard training, and results. Ponies were for winning competitions, not enjoying.

Alexia had never been in one place long enough to make proper friends, and Joe's rigorous training schedule left little time for a social life. But perhaps Seven Birches would change all that. She was starting at her new school the following day, and although she felt nervous, she was also excited about the prospect of meeting new people. It was a shame that she had already missed the start of term, thanks to Joe's hectic schedule, but hopefully that wouldn't matter. She drew herself tall and smiled brightly at her stepfather; not letting him know how she really felt, as usual.

Taking a deep breath, she followed him down the yard, determined to make this new chapter of her life a good one…

Chapter One

"Lily ... I'm over here."

The little palomino pony lifted her head from grazing and whinnied when she caught sight of Georgia sitting on the stone wall.

Georgia smiled. Lily had grown plump. Her golden coat shone with good health and her amber eyes were bright and alert. But there was something else... Lily's tummy was growing larger by the day, and Georgia had a feeling that it wasn't just to do with Redgrove Farm's rich summer grazing.

"How are you today, my beauty?" Georgia jumped down from the wall and walked across the Haydens' field. Melanie and Simon Hayden were the owners of the farm where Lily lived and they had helped Georgia rescue the palomino a few weeks' ago. Georgia sighed, rubbing the back of her arms in the cool afternoon breeze.

"Hey there!" A cheerful voice called out, rousing Georgia from her thoughts. Georgia spun round. It was Dan Coleman.

"Hello." She smiled shyly.

Dan and Georgia went to school together and had been firm friends ever since Lily had arrived at the yard. Georgia would always be grateful for the part that Dan had played in rescuing the little Welsh pony. As he strolled through the field now, the early autumn sunshine bouncing off his sandy-coloured hair, Georgia felt a buzz flood through her. He was a good-looking boy and his light blue eyes were set off by his cornflower-coloured jumper. Briefly she remembered the romantic moment they'd shared at the end-of-summer dance last month, then she pulled herself together. This was Dan she was talking about. Her *friend* Dan.

"So how's it going?' he asked, smiling back at Georgia as he came to stand beside her.

"It's going good,' she said shyly. "But Lily's getting fat." She chewed on a thumbnail. "I'm wondering if we could have brought back two ponies instead of one."

"Two?" Dan looked momentarily confused, before realisation spread crossed his face. "You mean, you think Lily could be *pregnant*?"

"I don't know for sure," Georgia said, brushing

her wavy blonde hair back from her face, and feeling suddenly nervous. "But I know someone who will!"

✩ ✩ ✩

A few days later, the local vet pulled up in his blue estate car. Georgia trusted him implicitly – Lily would have died of colic on the very night they'd rescued her if it hadn't been for him. Georgia knew she owed him Lily's life.

"There you are, Edward." Melanie Hayden strode out of the house with a tray laden with tea and chocolate biscuits. She was in her late forties, tall and slim.

"Melanie, the best tea maker on my rounds!" The vet grinned, accepting a steaming mug and a couple of biscuits. "So, where's the patient?"

"Over here," said Georgia, leading him to the far corner of the yard where Lily had been stabled for the night.

the
PALOMINO
✿PONY

The palomino pony was standing quietly inside, her molten eyes calmly taking in her surroundings.

"Hello, girl." The vet rubbed his hand over her glossy flanks. "Well, she's certainly looking great," he said. "So, pregnant, huh? You really think she could be?"

"Well, she has been getting larger by the minute." Melanie leaned in over the stable door.

"Let's take a look, then," said the vet. "See what we can find."

He was soon setting up the scanning equipment next to Lily while she observed him calmly. He listened to her heartbeat and took her temperature before running the monitor over the little mare's bulging stomach.

Georgia held her breath and Lily shifted her weight from her hindquarters as the vet examined the fuzzy picture on the screen carefully. Then he put a finger to his lips and beckoned Georgia over.

She knelt down, gazing at the image. All she could see was a confusing blur, and she couldn't make out exactly what she was looking at.

"Can you see that?" The vet pointed to a gently moving mass in the centre of the picture. "You were right, Georgia," he said. "Your little lady is in foal, and at a guess, I would say she's almost nine months."

"Nine months!" Georgia gave a gasp, which turned into a squeal. "So she's going to have a foal any second!"

The vet grinned. "Not quite any second. A horse's gestation period is longer than a human's. I'll do some further tests, but at a good guess I'd say that Lily will have a winter foal. Maybe early November."

Georgia exhaled slowly. It wasn't often that she was speechless but it took her a few minutes before she was able to regain her composure. Emotion welled up inside her. Lily … her very own Lily was carrying a precious bundle. Then a horrible thought struck her. "But, but I RODE her," she gasped, guilt crashing down on her. "She even jumped a fence when she saved me!"

The vet patted Lily's golden neck. "It's not ideal," he agreed. "But it doesn't look as though it's done her any damage. You weren't to know she was pregnant, Georgia. She was so thin when she came here. Now that she's being properly fed and looked after, well … she's blooming. I wouldn't worry – just don't ride her any more. You can take her out in hand instead, like you were doing when your wrist was fractured. She'd enjoy that."

He gave Georgia a warm, reassuring smile. She'd actually only ridden Lily a few times as she'd had a fall that had left her wrist in plaster for three weeks, and then she'd had to wait until the physio allowed her to start riding again. If the vet said that Lily and her foal were fine then she would take his word for it.

"Lily's going to have a foal!" Georgia repeated the words, a wide grin breaking out on her face. "Just wait till I tell Mum!"

"I wonder who the father could be," Melanie mused. "She was out in that mountainside paddock for quite some time."

"Well, let's just hope it was a nice Welsh stallion," the vet said. "The most important thing is that she's here now. And she and her foal are in excellent hands!"

Chapter Two

Later that day, once Lily had been turned out into her field and Georgia had tidied the yard, she sprinted the half mile or so down the road to Dan's farm. He lived with his dad and brother, Ben. Knocking on the door, she hopped excitedly from foot to foot.

"Hey, Georgia. Come on in." Dan finally pulled back the door, running a hand wearily through his hair. He looked pale and was wearing an old jumper and jeans. "I've just got in from the milking. Do you want something to drink? Juice?"

"I'm fine, thanks," said Georgia, stepping inside.

"Have you just come from the yard?"

"Yes!" Georgia couldn't contain herself any longer. "And you'll never guess what. I was right! Lily's in foal!" Georgia's words spilled out, one after the other.

A slow smile spread across Dan's face, lighting it up. "Hey Georgia, that's brilliant! Lily will be an excellent mum."

"I know," Georgia chattered on, excitement bubbling over. "I can't quite believe it! I've never seen a foal up close before. I wonder if I can watch it being born!"

Dan laughed. "Well, I've seen plenty of calves being born, and let me tell you, it's not a pretty sight. Still, there's something special about a new birth, and Lily will want you there, for sure."

"Thanks, Dan." Georgia smiled. "Now, maybe I will have that juice…"

☆ ☆ ☆

School had come around far too quickly, after the best summer holidays ever, and although they were now a few weeks into term. Georgia still felt glum on Monday mornings. She and her best friend, Emma, were in Year Nine now, which meant even more coursework. Georgia hated every second of it, but she was trying to keep up. There was no way she wanted to end up on another crammer course, even if the last one had led her to Wales and to Lily!

At last, the school week came to an end and Georgia packed her things away before heading for the bus. When she walked up the drive to Redgrove and pushed open the door, Melanie was already sitting at the kitchen table, tapping away at her laptop.

"Just emailing Sophie, G," she said, looking up. "She seems to be settling well into university life."

"That's great," grinned Georgia, thinking about Melanie's daughter. Tall and slim with long blonde hair, Sophie was a brilliant rider. She'd only just gone to uni and Georgia missed her. They had grown closer recently. The night before Sophie had left she had even made a tearful plea to Georgia to look after her horse, Wilson, for her. Georgia had been as good as her word and had texted her every day, often sending a funny photo of Wilson to cheer her up. Which reminded her…

"Is it all right if I go out on to the yard?" she asked.

"Sure," Melanie answered. "I'll come and join you in a minute. Lily could do with a groom before we bring the others in for their evening feed."

"OK," Georgia answered.

When Georgia stepped out, she saw Lily waiting by her gate for her. The palomino gave a small whicker.

"Lily, my angel..." Georgia ran a hand over the pony's small neat head before burying her face in her neck and breathing in her wonderful scent. The night air was cool and overcast. Slipping Lily's headcollar on over her nose, she led her into the yard where she was going to groom her.

"I'm going to give you the best make-over ever," she crooned.

This was Georgia's favourite part of horse care and tonight was no exception. She curry-combed, body-brushed and polished until Lily's golden coat was positively gleaming.

"There," she said finally as she stood back to admire her handiwork. "Now – time for your supper."

As Lily buried her head in the bucket of feed,

Georgia sat quietly, watching her eat. Georgia still couldn't quite believe Lily was hers – on loan to her from Melanie, but otherwise her very own pony. And every moment with the palomino was turning out to be so precious…

✩ ✩ ✩

Later that evening, after supper with Mum, Georgia curled up in bed with her foaling book, rereading the chapters over and over again. There was so much to take in and so much to learn! Closing her eyes and turning on to her side, Georgia clutched the book to her chest. In no time at all, Lily would be having a baby! It was terrifying but exciting too.

Georgia sighed, and with her head filled with dreams of ponies and foals, she fell fast asleep.

CHAPTER THREE

The next morning, when Georgia woke, she couldn't get up to Redgrove quickly enough. Weekends were special as she got to spend the whole day at the yard. She was sitting in the kitchen having a cup of tea and cleaning tack with Melanie when the phone rang.

"Georgia, it's Janey," Melanie said, holding out the phone to her. "She wants a word with you.

Something about the Round Barrow team."

Georgia jumped up, puzzled. Janey was Sophie's riding instructor and the head of the local Pony Club team. She didn't usually call to speak to her. Georgia rubbed a streak of saddle soap from her forehead, her dark blonde hair falling across her face, and took the phone.

"Hello, Janey," she said politely.

"Georgia, great, I thought I would find you at Mel's." Janey spoke fast, in a clipped, no-nonsense tone. "Now listen, I wanted to talk to you about something. I need another rider for the Show Pony Autumn Championships – in the Working Hunter Team Challenge – what with Tory, um, not available any more."

Georgia listened intently. Tory was Sophie's ex-best friend. Since they'd found out that she'd been partly responsible for the attempted theft of Lily, she and Sophie hadn't been so close. Still, Georgia didn't want to think about that now. She tried to tune into what Janey was saying instead.

"So," the riding instructor continued smoothly, "I was wondering if you wanted to try out? Melanie tells me you're making great progress."

"Me?" Georgia squeaked, hardly able to contain her excitement. She – Georgia Black – was being invited to try out for the Round Barrow team! She wanted to pinch herself to check that she wasn't dreaming. Janey was still talking. "There will be a few people trying out, of course, but lots of the girls have got other stuff going on and we need commitment. I know you work hard at Mel's and she's always telling me what a naturally gifted rider you are."

Georgia blushed. She turned to stare at Melanie who was busy peeling carrots, smiling to herself. "Go on," Melanie mouthed.

"So what do you think?" the voice came from

the other end of the phone. "Are you still there?"

"Er … yes, I mean … er…" Quickly pulling herself together, Georgia cleared her throat. "Oh my goodness, really?" she said, kicking herself for sounding so nervous.

"Yes, of course," said Janey. "I'm not promising anything, though," she finished, rather more matter-of-factly.

"Yes, yes of course," said Georgia. "So what day should I be there?" She paused. "OK, yes, next Saturday should be just fine. Ten o'clock sharp at yours. Oh but…" Suddenly something struck Georgia. She couldn't take part. How could she when Lily was in foal? She didn't have a pony to ride.

As if reading her thoughts, Janey continued. "Mel's said you can ride Wilson – now that Sophie's away."

"Wilson!" Georgia drew her breath in sharply,

22

turning to look at Mel who laughed.

"Can't have a perfectly good horse out in the field while he could be jumping on the team," Janey continued. "And congratulations on Lily, always liked that mare. Did she come to you in foal?"

"Yes!" Georgia squeaked excitedly, her face lighting up as it did every time she remembered Lily's baby. And before she could stop herself, she was chatting nineteen-to-the-dozen about the foal's progress and Lily's future as a mum. After nearly ten minutes, Janey interrupted with a chuckle. "Sorry, Georgia," she said, "normally I would love to hear all about it but I've got to go…"

"Sure…" As Georgia put down the phone, she saw the look on Mel's face. "You knew!" she cried.

"Of course I knew!" said Mel.

"And you're sure it's all right?" said Georgia.

"For me to borrow Wilson, I mean. Sophie won't mind?"

"Of course she doesn't mind," said Mel. "I've already asked her and she's delighted. The poor old boy's been missing his competitions while she's been away. She's pleased that someone's going to be exercising him. Besides, you'll be trying out for the junior team, not the seniors, so it won't conflict with Sophie..." She smiled at Georgia. "So, what do you think?"

It took all of Georgia's willpower not to jump up and down and squeal. "I can't thank you enough!" she cried, her stomach already churning with nerves and excitement.

"OK then!" said Melanie. "We'd better put in some practice this week!"

Georgia couldn't stop grinning from ear to ear as she assembled the bridle she'd just finished cleaning. She was so lucky to have Redgrove!

CHAPTER FOUR

For once, Georgia couldn't wait to climb aboard the school bus on Monday. She was bursting to share the news of the trials with her best friend, Emma. She had resisted the urge to text her as she'd wanted to tell her in person. But, as she got on, her friend's usual seat was empty. That was strange. Em always got in touch if she was ill or if her mum was dropping her off at school. Still, she'd probably just forgotten.

Settling into her seat, Georgia stared out of the window and soon she was lost in thought – imagining jumping every hedge and fence in sight as the countryside rolled past. It was only when Dan boarded a few stops later and took the empty seat next to her that she looked up.

"Hey!" she grinned, noticing a piece of straw still in his hair and carefully removing it.

"Hey back!" He prodded her playfully on the arm. "Where's Em?"

"I don't know," replied Georgia. "She didn't say anything yesterday about feeling ill."

"Maybe she's with Lexie?" suggested Dan.

"Lexie?" Georgia puzzled. "Who's she?"

Dan chuckled. "Honestly, Georgia. Do you not notice anything at school?"

Georgia thought hard.

"You can't have missed her," Dan started again.

"New girl. Tall and slim. She's pretty cool. Sat at the back of the class yesterday – dark brown hair."

"Sorry, you've got me there." Georgia shrugged. "Still, I guess I'll get to meet her soon enough."

"It's even weirder that you didn't notice her, seeing as she's really into horses too," said Dan.

"Horses?" Georgia's ears pricked up. "Really?"

"Yes, really," said Dan. "Her dad's just bought that big new yard up by Beecher's Wood – Seven Birches."

"The one with the indoor arena and stuff?" said Georgia.

"The very one," said Dan.

"I can't believe it!" said Georgia. "Wasn't that owned by a German dressage rider?"

"Yep," said Dan. "Lexie's stepdad's paid a fortune for it, apparently."

Georgia was suddenly more interested in the new girl. "I'll definitely have to meet her then. So how does Em know her?"

"From when they were younger, I think," said Dan. "Their dads know each other. Anyway, come on, we're here."

The school bus lurched to a stop outside some red-brick buildings and they all jumped off. As they headed for the main entrance, a sleek grey four-by-four pulled up next to them.

"Georgia!" A familiar voice cried and a girl with long dark hair bounded out of the car.

"Em!" Georgia cried. "Why weren't you on the bus?"

A girl stepped out behind her. Georgia guessed it must be Lexie.

"I got a lift with Lexie," Emma said, falling into step beside Georgia. "Sorry, I should've let you know. My dad and Lexie's dad had some business stuff to do this morning so Lexie's dad said he would drop us off first. Oh, sorry – Georgia, this is

Lexie. Lexie meet Georgia."

Lexie smiled and Georgia grinned back. She was tall, probably taller even than Dan, and had a sleek bob of dark brown hair that glinted as she tossed her head and held out her hand. "Hey," she said in a voice that had a distinctive Yorkshire accent. "Emma's been telling me all about you and your ponies, Lily and Wilson."

"Well, they're not exactly *my* ponies, as such," Georgia explained. "Lily's mine on loan and Wilson – well, I'm just looking after him while his owner's at university."

"Still, it's pretty cool," said Lexie. "And Emma told me how you rescued one of them. That's so amazing!"

"Well, thank you!" said Georgia, blushing with pride and instantly warming to the girl. And she could see why Dan had described her as cool. Not only was Lexie super-pretty, with her shiny hair and smooth, tanned skin, but she was self-assured and confident too, far more so than any of the other Year Nines who were staring at them as they filed past.

"Dan said your dad has bought the place up by Beecher's," said Georgia. "And that you like ponies." She was aware that her voice sounded croaky and young all of a sudden.

Lexie nodded. "I love ponies, sure – but if you've heard about the competing, well that's my stepdad's thing, really."

"Oh." Georgia was surprised by the change in Lexie's voice. She had sounded – well, steely somehow, and after being so friendly. Georgia opened her mouth to say something but in a flash Lexie grinned, warmth flooding back into her features. "You should come over sometime."

Georgia grinned back. "I'd love to," she said. "Thanks very much!"

☆ ☆ ☆

Later that day, as the bell rang for the end of school, Georgia bumped into Emma coming out of her maths class. She tucked her arm into her friend's and they walked in silence for a few steps.

"Is everything OK, G?" Emma said finally.

"Yes!" Georgia said in surprise. "Why wouldn't it be?"

Emma shrugged. "You've just been in your own little world all day, that's all. I was worried you might be cross that I came to school in Lexie's car."

"Don't be silly, Em." Georgia hugged her friend. "Not at all! But I've got something to tell you. I've been saving it up all day – ever since you weren't on the bus."

"Ooh, what is it?" asked Emma.

"It's the Working Hunter Team Challenge at the Autumn Championships!" Georgia squealed. "Janey rang me at the weekend to ask if I'd try out for it!"

"But that's brilliant, G!" Emma squealed back, hugging her friend. Then she went a little quiet. "You never know – one day, I might even be able to try out with you."

"Oh, Em…" said Georgia, feeling a little sad that her friend wasn't going to be doing it too. But Em wasn't much more than a beginner – she'd only just started riding at Mel's recently when she'd had a few lessons on Wilson.

"Hang on, there's Lexie," said Emma. "Let's tell her!"

"No, Em, stop…" Georgia's voice trailed off.

But it was too late. Em was already rushing off and had joined Lexie on the other side of the playground. Georgia sighed. It was going to sound so stupid when she hadn't even been picked yet. Especially when Lexie had so many ponies of her own. Georgia felt embarrassed as she caught up with the two girls.

Emma turned to her. "Guess what!" she cried. "Lexie's trying out as well."

"Yes, I am." Lexie nodded in agreement, but her face darkened once again as she spoke. Georgia looked at her in surprise but just as quickly as before, Lexie regained her composure. "Are you still coming round tonight, Em?" she asked in a cheerful voice.

"You bet!" Em grinned before turning to Georgia. "You don't mind, do you?" she asked. "I know I said I was going to come and see Lily but Lexie has invited me over and her dad, sorry Lexie, *stepdad* has invited my dad over so that's why I'm going too..."

Georgia felt a little wave of jealousy creeping up inside but she quickly pushed it away. Em was her best friend and nothing was going to change that. Of course she should take up the chance of going over to the yard! She grinned. "Don't be silly, Em," she smiled. "Don't worry at all! I'll see you tomorrow."

"Cool," said Emma, looking relieved.

Georgia watched as, just at that moment, Lexie's stepdad swept up again in his silver car, opening the door for the girls in a flourish. He had a well-groomed, monied appearance. Looking at his suit and shoes, there was no way Georgia could imagine him mucking out!

☆ ☆ ☆

Boarding the school bus, Georgia looked around for Dan's familiar face but she couldn't spot him anywhere. Sighing, she turned on her mobile and it bleeped instantly with a message.

Sorry, G, my dad picked me up. Farm emergency. D.

That was strange. She knew that Dan and his brother, Ben, ran a tight ship when it came to the farm and farm shop. She hoped it was nothing too serious. As the bus rattled down the roads and made the turn to Redgrove, Georgia was lost in her thoughts. She was pleased to finally find herself walking up the drive and looking out over the fields.

"There's a girl," Georgia called to Lily.

Lily was grazing in the small front paddock with Callie, a small Exmoor pony. Callie was retired now, but Sophie had once competed on her at the Horse of the Year Show and at Olympia. Now, she was quietly grazing with Lily, nose to nose, occasionally pausing to flick some drowsy flies from her companion's face with her tail. Callie had been devoted to the palomino pony ever since her dramatic arrival at the yard. And Callie seemed to see it as her duty to mother her more than ever now that she was pregnant.

The evening was unexpectedly warm. Georgia caught Lily with a small handful of pony nuts and slipped the headcollar on over her nose. Tying her up in the yard she set about grooming her. Pregnancy had given Lily's coat an extra sheen.

Lily closed her eyes and her bottom lip drooped as Georgia brushed her coat. It always amazed her just how trusting Lily was, considering her past. She really was one extra-special pony!

CHAPTER FIVE

The next day at school, Georgia ate her lunch with Lexie and Emma. The two of them were giggling over something but Georgia wasn't really paying attention. As Dan joined them, throwing his battered school bag down and pulling out his food, she smiled at him. He looked tired and deflated and didn't make conversation, staring straight ahead as he chewed on his sandwich.

"Dan?" Georgia asked him eventually. "Are you OK?"

Dan raked a hand through his unkempt curly hair. "Just about," he said. "It's the farm, that's all."

Georgia gave him a look and he smiled weakly. "We're just in a bit of a tight spot at the moment," he explained. "Nothing that we haven't faced before, though."

Georgia didn't really understand farming, but she knew that Dan and his dad and brother kept sheep and cows. Their farm shop was extremely popular and people came from far and wide to buy everything from cheese and meat to biscuits and cakes.

"Been practising for Saturday, Georgia?" Lexie's friendly voice broke into her thoughts and she looked up to see Lexie smiling at her.

"A bit," Georgia said. "Mel gives me lessons

when she has time but mostly I just jump things when I'm out hacking. We made some cool straw bale jumps last week, didn't we, Em?"

Emma nodded. "It was such fun, Lexie. You should come out with us soon!"

Lexie laughed, but it sounded a little hollow. "Joe would never let me." She bit her bottom lip. "The ponies are far too valuable."

"What? For hacking?" Georgia said in an incredulous voice. "You mean, they just stay in the school? All the time?"

"Yup," Lexie said. "No hacking out for me. And I've got to qualify for the Horse of the Year Show this year or Joe's going to flip."

Georgia was startled. She had learned from Emma that Lexie's stepdad was very driven but she couldn't imagine having that sort of pressure. Georgia's mum wasn't horsey at all. She couldn't tell a hoof pick from a hock but she was always interested in Georgia's news about Redgrove. It was hard to imagine what it would be like if her enjoyment of being around the ponies was tainted by being pushed to do well in competitions.

CHAPTER SIX

The morning of the trials dawned bright and cold with a faint acidic smell in the air. A low silver mist clung to the fields as Georgia trudged through the wet grass with Wilson's headcollar. She paused to stroke Lily, who nuzzled her head against her quilted jacket, leaving a grassy mark. Georgia chuckled and brushed it off before slipping the headcollar over Wilson's nose. He was just starting to lose his summer coat and his dark brown sides had taken on a lustrous velvet appearance.

"Come on, Wilson. In we go..." Georgia ran her hand through his mane and quietly clucked under her breath for him to walk on. Lily trotted alongside and Georgia laid a hand on her shoulder. Her heart swelled with love for the sweet golden mare and, all over again, she felt excitement at the arrival of the foal bubble up inside her. She couldn't wait!

The journey to Janey's was quiet. Georgia tried to suppress her growing nerves. Her stomach was churning and she dug her nails into her palm as she tried to remember what Mel had taught her.

"Sit up, look ahead, give Wilson his head," she muttered under her breath. She knew that the brave brown pony was experienced and could do his job. She just hoped she didn't mess it up for him!

As they pulled into Janey's immaculate yard, Georgia felt her stomach lurch. Gulping in the cool air as she swung open the lorry door, she looked around the parking area. There was Lottie, who was in her last year of pony club before she took up a place to study veterinary medicine, then a girl Georgia didn't recognise with a perky-looking black pony who whinnied at their arrival, and...

Oh no. Georgia gave a groan. It was Harry, the most arrogant boy in the pony club. As usual, he was laughing loudly, leaning up against his horsebox as his mother, with pearls around her neck bigger than a set of marbles, flitted around, tacking up his horse, Hector. As she passed Harry a can of Coke, he spotted Georgia and winked. "Gross," she muttered under her breath.

Then, out of the corner of her eye, Georgia caught sight of the biggest horsebox she had ever seen. It was so long that, for a moment, she thought it might not be able to take the corner through the gates. But with some skilful manoeuvring, the huge silver and black vehicle purred into the yard. Someone immediately opened the passenger door. Lexie!

Even Harry turned his head and gaped as Lexie swung out of the cab, landing gracefully. She was wearing cream jodhpurs and the softest-looking riding boots Georgia had ever seen.

Nudging Georgia, Harry pointed to the box. "Sponsorship and everything," he said, awe-struck. Georgia noticed the initials DD intertwined and emblazoned on the side of the lorry in silver and black.

A whippet-slim man climbed out of the driver's seat and looked around. *Who was he?* Georgia wondered. It wasn't Lexie's stepdad. Maybe he was one of Lexie's trainers? She had heard Emma talk about the staff employed at Seven Birches.

Georgia gave Lexie a small wave as she unloaded Wilson, and Lexie gave her a half-smile back before busying herself with her jacket buttons. She looked pale and anxious.

Georgia couldn't work Lexie out. Sometimes she was so friendly and confident and then, at what seemed like a flick of a switch, she was a different person.

Oh well. Turning back to Wilson, Georgia unbuckled the straps of his rugs. She was just crouching down to take off his dark green travel boots when she heard a familiar voice.

"Georgia!"

It was Emma! Georgia jumped to her feet to greet her friend. She'd had no idea Emma was coming today. "What are you doing here?" she asked. She didn't meant it to sound unwelcoming, but it sort of did.

"Sorry, G," Emma said quickly. "I didn't realise

I had to ask your permission."

Georgia stepped back, feeling stung. "No, no, of course not," she said. "I didn't mean it like that. It's just ... well, I just thought you were busy today, that's all."

Emma must have realized that she had sounded blunt, as her tone instantly softened as well. "I was going to go shopping," she said carefully. "But Lexie needed a bit of support because – well, because her stepdad's not with her today, and…" She smiled awkwardly and seemed about to say more, but then she stopped herself. "Anyway, Dad said I should come along to help."

"Oh, cool," Georgia replied, trying to sound nonchalant. "So who is that guy with her?"

Emma put her hands over her eyes and squinted into the early autumn sunlight. "Over there? Oh, that's Mike. Or is it Jason?" she said. "I don't know – I muddle up the trainers. They're all so similar."

"Trainers?" Georgia couldn't believe her ears. "As in *more* than one?"

Emma rolled her eyes. "And the rest." She counted on her fingers. "Two trainers, two grooms I think, oh and Ray, the handy man. He does the fencing and stuff. And Lisa, she rides the ponies when Lexie's at school."

"Wow!" said Georgia, secretly impressed. There didn't seem much else to say. She felt a little tingle of excitement flood through her. She couldn't wait to visit Seven Birches at some point. It sounded amazing! She just hoped that Lexie would remember she'd invited her.

As if reading her thoughts Emma spoke. "Lexie's stepdad is quite funny about who visits the yard, you know. I think he only lets me 'cos Dad is something to do with his business."

"Oh right," said Georgia, feeling a little put-down, though she didn't know exactly why.

"So what does he do for Lexie's dad?" she asked curiously.

Emma shrugged. "Don't know exactly," she replied. "You know Dad works in property law, and Lexie's stepdad is something to do with property, so..."

"Oh. Right." Georgia nodded, not really any the wiser.

"Georgia," Emma said in a hesitant voice. "There's something I need to talk to you about."

Georgia looked questioningly at Em. It sounded serious.

Emma took a deep breath. "Lexie's offered me riding lessons at Seven Birches," she said finally.

"Oh," Georgia said.

"What do you think?" asked Em.

"But you've been having lessons at Mel's. How are you going to do both?" said Georgia.

"Well, that's just it," Emma replied. "I can't be in

48

two places at once, and as I can't really ride Wilson if you need to practise all the time, it seems like a good idea to just have them at Seven Birches."

Georgia didn't know what to say.

What Emma said was true but her heart still sank. She'd been enjoying riding with Emma at Redgrove, especially with Sophie away at the moment. Emma was slowly building up confidence and Georgia would miss her being around. Then, suddenly, something struck her. "But you don't need to ride Wilson. Mel was going to ask about borrowing that cob gelding from the local riding school. The one that was going to be semi-retired, remember?"

"Yeah, well, Lexie's got plenty of ponies for me to ride," Emma said nonchalantly.

"Oh right," said Georgia, surprised. "Well, I guess you'd better just tell Mel then." She took a deep breath and was about to say more but, at that moment, she heard Lexie calling Emma's name. The next minute she came clattering over on her pony.

Georgia was instantly wowed by the gelding. He was the whitest shade of snow, apart from a splattering of black appaloosa spots and a few black streaks in his thick tail that gave him an other-worldly appearance. A grackle bridle in the softest shade of Havana emphasised his fine features as he pricked his curved ears and gazed with interest at the jumps that were being set up in the outdoor arena.

Lexie sat quietly in the saddle, her contact soft and light. "So glad you came, Em," she said, ignoring Georgia. She nudged her pony around and guided him towards the arena, followed by Emma who gave a guilty glance in Georgia's direction.

"Catch up soon, G," she said, before laughing at

something Georgia couldn't quite hear.

Georgia felt dejected. She knew Emma was a kind-hearted girl who liked to make people feel welcome, but Georgia felt she was being left behind. And, try as she might, she couldn't snuff out the small flame of jealousy that had ignited inside her.

CHAPTER SEVEN

Georgia turned her attention to Wilson. She patted his sleek brown neck before tacking him up in a simple snaffle bridle and working hunter saddle with a dark brown sheepskin underneath. She had just finished putting on his front boots, when Melanie came back from chatting with another pony-club mum. Melanie legged her into the saddle.

"Easy now, Wilson," Georgia breathed. She always felt small on the 14.2 gelding who rode more like a 16h horse. Nudging him gently with her heels, she joined the rest of the riders who were lining up in the centre of the arena.

Janey strode in, her short grey curls bouncing and a terrier hanging on to the riding crop in her hand. "Right, kids, listen up," she boomed and even Harry stopped chatting to the red-headed girl next to him. "I'm looking for four riders today," she continued, studying each and every one of them in turn. "Good luck, and let's get going!"

Georgia took a deep breath. The trial was fairly straightforward. After warming up, the riders were going to jump a course of rustic jumps, including a water jump. Georgia felt her stomach flip as she looked at the course. The fences were about three feet high but they were solid. She walked Wilson around the perimeter of the arena, concentrating on working him long and low as Melanie had taught her.

Harry was ambling along next to her, riding aimlessly on a long rein and attempting to talk to her. Georgia tried to ignore him. Her teeth were chattering too much. She was third to jump, behind Harry and Lexie.

Her eyes narrowed as she watched Lexie cantering her pony on a twenty-metre circle. She had to hand it to her, she was a fantastic rider. Her reins were soft and light, and the appaloosa pony looked relaxed and happy. Her seat didn't move in the saddle as she brought him back to walk, changed the rein and went into a perfect walk-canter transition on the other rein. The trainer that had accompanied her put up a small cross pole and called for her to jump it.

Lexie circled close to Georgia. Georgia glanced at her as they passed. Lexie's mouth was set in a thin line and her dark eyes flashed in a suddenly white face. Her poise was stiff and her elbows clenched. If Georgia didn't know better she would have thought that Lexie looked terrified. She felt a wave of sympathy for her as she watched her pop over the small jump. Although her position was still text-book perfect, all the natural grace had disappeared as she circled back towards the second jump that her trainer had put up.

Again, her pony jumped it neatly, but by now it really was obvious that Lexie was scared. Georgia also circled and jumped the small jump next to her. Lexie turned towards her, her face paler than her pony's white coat and hissed at Georgia.

"Keep your pony away! He'll spook River."

Georgia was so startled she didn't have time to reply.

Then Lexie's trainer was beside her, and she was leaving the warm-up as he barked instructions.

Emma was scurrying behind, holding the grooming kit.

Still, there wasn't time to think about that now. Lexie was the first to go in to the arena.

"Keep a straight line!" Janey called across to her.

One … two … three … and take-off. Lexie jumped the first fence perfectly. Now it was on to the double. One … two … and over. Lexie jumped beautifully around the course. Georgia admired the way she kept a soft contact the whole way round, never once jabbing River in the mouth, moving in one fluid motion. But as she took the final fence and brought River down to a walk, Georgia noticed with a shock that Lexie's eyes were brimming with tears.

Lexie's trainer took hold of River's bridle and led him out as Lexie sat, stone-still.

Georgia glanced at Emma, who was leaning over the arena fence. "What's going on?" she asked.

Emma shrugged. "Lexie's just nervous about letting her stepdad down, I think."

"Hmmm." Georgia wasn't so sure. She was convinced she had seen real fear in Lexie's eyes, and that was far from ideal when trying out for a competitive team…

CHAPTER EIGHT

Harry was next into the ring with Hector. The skewbald had an air of resignation about him as he circled, waiting for the imaginary bell. He was a kind horse and tried his best at all times. Despite his size and his dinner-plate sized hooves, he also jumped a stylish clear round. Harry wasn't a pretty rider by any means, but Hector more than made up for all of his faults. Even when Harry put him into fences on the wrong stride or didn't give with his hands enough, Hector managed to correct the errors. Once again, Georgia marvelled at his generous nature. Harry was very lucky to own such a sweet, honest horse. Harry smirked at her as he exited the arena.

"Good luck, shorty," he grinned.

Georgia shot him a look. Harry could be so annoying at times. Dan's weary face flashed in front of her and she wished he was here instead of Harry. She made a mental note to visit him later to check he was all right.

"OK, Georgia!" Janey's shrill voice cut across her thoughts. "Off you go when you're ready. I'll pretend to be the bell – ding-a-ling – good luck!"

Georgia swallowed hard, sat up straight, and nudged Wilson into a forward canter. She circled the arena before approaching the first jump, an upright gate. Wilson pricked his ears and flew over it, before instantly locking eyes on to the next jump. Fence after fence disappeared under his black hooves.

Georgia started to relax, laughing and enjoying the round. The third-to-last fence was the water jump. Georgia had only tried this once at home, over Melanie's homemade black tarpaulin, filled from the yard hose. But this was much bigger, and horribly wide.

Feeling her hesitation, Wilson checked as he cantered up to it, just as Georgia gave him a determined nudge with her heels. The mixed message sent him over-jumping from two strides out, and he stumbled on landing.

Georgia clung on to his neck but not tightly enough and before she knew it, she felt the ground rushing up to meet her. She landed on her shoulder, still clutching a startled Wilson's bridle. Jumping to her feet she hugged the bay pony over

PALOMINO PONY

and over, totally mortified.

Janey was beside her in a flash. "Legs? Arms?" she demanded, checking Georgia hadn't broken anything.

Totally dejected, Georgia shook her head. She was all right but she had clearly blown it.

"Well, get back on then!" Janey bellowed with an authoritarian air. "You don't want to lose your nerve!"

Gingerly, Georgia did as she was told and remounted, wiping her face with the back of her hand. The other riders were blurry through her tears but she thought she saw Lexie shoot her a look of sympathy before her face closed up again. Under Janey's watchful eye, Georgia circled the jump. This time she rode it perfectly, and jumped the last two fences with ease.

Walking out of the arena, Georgia tried not to look at the other riders. Harry was grinning at her and mouthing "Ouch," but Lexie was sitting quietly, not saying a thing. Luckily Melanie bounded over, taking hold of Wilson's bridle and patting his neck.

"Mel, I..." Georgia began, her voice trembling.

"Don't worry about it," Melanie said firmly. "The main thing is that you got back on and completed the course. You did brilliantly."

Georgia felt a wave of relief flood through her at Melanie's kind words. They untacked Wilson together, and Georgia gave him a mint. Once he was safely tied back in the lorry with a hay net, Georgia and Melanie made their way back to the arena.

A small blonde girl was just finishing her round on a gangly chestnut thoroughbred, scattering poles everywhere. The horse did at least five laps of the arena before she was able to pull him up, an embarrassed smile on her face. *At least I wasn't the*

only one, Georgia thought to herself.

The next three riders had slightly better luck, and ended up with just two refusals, and six poles down between them. So far, only Lexie and Harry had jumped clear, but no one had fallen off apart from Georgia. She took a seat at the side of the arena to wait for Janey's verdict. Her shoulder was aching and she could feel a bruise developing on her hip. She was aware of someone leaning over the fence, watching the proceedings. Who was he? He looked kind of familiar. And then Georgia realised where she had seen him before. It was Lexie's stepdad.

As Lexie walked over to him, she looked pensive and miserable. And yet she had jumped the perfect round.

The riders huddled around the fence, joking and chatting among themselves. Emma, who had smiled sympathetically when Georgia completed her round, stood with Lexie, looking slightly awkward as Joe was clearly giving his stepdaughter a lecture. If Georgia wasn't mistaken, he looked really mad. She wished Emma would just come over and see her but she guessed she didn't want to leave her new friend's side as her reason for coming along had been to give her moral support.

Janey strode into the arena with an elderly man in a flat cap, who looked as though he had been born on a horse. A plump Jack Russell waddled leisurely by his side.

"Listen up, everyone…" Janey's voiced boomed out. "This is Hugh," she said. Georgia suddenly recognised him as a famous show judge.

As one, all of the pony-club members and their families turned towards Janey expectantly as she consulted the list in her hand.

Melanie patted Georgia on the shoulder. "Try not to worry, G," she said.

Janey stepped forward, clearing her throat. "Hugh and I have talked about this carefully," she said, her hands on her hip. "Some of you rode well, others... Well, let's just say we were disappointed."

Georgia blushed scarlet. She knew she meant her. Janey was starting to speak again.

"So, here's what we've decided – Lexie, you're a definite for the team. Harry – you too. You rode a lovely round." Janey paused. "We've also decided that Lottie has made the team."

Lottie gave a small whoop of delight. Her pony, Songbird, was a real star. Georgia felt her hopes fade further. Then Janey looked directly at her. "This was a hard decision," she said. "But we chose the fourth rider for her potential. Hugh felt that she showed a lot of guts." Janey looked down her list, the suspense among the riders growing unbearably before she looked up again and smiled.

"Georgia Black, you're our fourth rider."

"Me?" Georgia gaped at her in astonishment. Melanie grinned.

She'd made the team! She felt a pang of guilt as she registered the disappointment on the other pony-club faces, but then she felt overcome with happiness. She had made the team! She couldn't believe it!

Janey was beside her in an instant. "Georgia, we know you fell at the water jump," she said. "But we chose you because you showed determination and style. We all fall sometimes – it's how you come out of it that matters."

Georgia couldn't keep the grin off her face for the rest of the day. The only cloud on the horizon was Emma. While she had genuinely congratulated Georgia when the names were read out, she had scuttled back to Lexie's box as soon as it was all over, to help her untack River. Georgia had tried not to feel rejected as her friend scurried around after Lexie, trailing bridles and rugs.

Lexie's stepdad was drumming his fingers on the steering wheel of the vast lorry, clearly keen to get moving. Georgia knew Emma was being friendly, and that she was the only person Lexie knew in Redgrove, but she would have liked to be with her. She couldn't remember a time she and Emma had been apart. It wasn't as if they were arguing even, but Emma was clearly getting caught up in Lexie's world – a world in which Georgia didn't feature. Still, nothing was going to ruin her triumph at making it on to the team!

CHAPTER NINE

That afternoon, Georgia heard a familiar whicker as she turned a grateful Wilson back out into the fields. It was another warm day and Lily was dozing in the shade of the chestnut tree, resting a leg, her bottom lip drooping as she closed her eyes. Callie was lying flat out beside her, her eyes firmly shut. As Georgia scratched Lily's neck she delighted at what good health the palomino was in. She was a far cry from the bedraggled, frightened pony she had once been.

Walking back to the yard, Georgia caught sight of Melanie leaning on the gate, wearing a battered pair of country boots tucked into faded jeans. She was tying up the spare lead ropes, but as Georgia approached she looked up and smiled. "I've got something I need to talk to you about," she said gently.

"Sounds serious," Georgia said immediately.

"Well it is, kind of," Mel replied kindly. "I was wondering – do you fancy taking a little road trip?"

"A road trip?" Georgia gave her a questioning look.

"We need to go to Wales," Mel finished.

"Wales!" Georgia sucked in her breath. It was where Lily had come from. "But why?" she asked, her heart sinking, knowing the answer already.

"It's only fair that we find out the sire of Lily's foal," said Melanie. "And I know Eric will be able to help."

Georgia nodded, thinking of the old man who'd once owned the Carlamu Show Stud, where Lily had come from. She knew it made sense, but she was worried she'd end up having to see his horrible granddaughter, Jemma. She was the one who'd mistreated Lily in the first place and then tried to steal her back. She was the last person Georgia wanted to meet.

"Are you worried about it, Georgia?" Melanie asked gently. "Because if you are, I can go on my own."

"No, no, I'll come with you," said Georgia.

"There's nothing to be concerned about," said Melanie. "Lily is officially ours now. I have the paperwork and after what happened with the police last time, Jemma isn't going to try anything."

"I know," said Georgia. She traced an "O" with the toe of her boot as she kept her head down. "I just always worry that having Lily is too good to be true and that she'll end up being taken away from me again."

"Georgia," Melanie gently chided. "That will never happen. I won't let it. She's your pony now. OK?"

Georgia smiled weakly. "OK," she agreed. "And let's go to Wales together, but only to see Eric!"

Melanie nodded. "Only Eric. I promise."

✿ ✿ ✿

The Colemans' farm was quiet as Georgia dropped by later that afternoon, the cows back out in their field before milking. Georgia was surprised that there was only one car in the normally busy shop car park. She leaned her bike against the wall of the bungalow and knocked on the door. Dan's older brother, Ben, answered, running a hand through his dirty blond hair, his feet bare on the worn stone of the porch. He looked tired and barely raised a smile at seeing Georgia.

"Hey, G," he said, letting her in. "Daniel's in the kitchen."

Dan gave her a wave from where he was sitting at the table, eating a piece of toast. The kitchen, once the centre of the home before the boys' mother had died, was now messy. Gone were the gleaming work surfaces and fresh flowers and in their place were endless piles of paperwork and half-empty coffee mugs.

Dan's eyes were puffy and his face was pale. He smiled weakly but Georgia couldn't help noticing the letters piled up on the kitchen table. They had angry red stamps on them with things like "FINAL DEMAND" and "IMPORTANT NOTICE".

Dan followed her gaze and hastily swept the letters aside.

"Dan, is everything OK?" Georgia asked, hesitatingly.

"Yes. Well, no, not really," Dan said. "We're just having trouble with the shop, that's all."

"The shop? But why?" Georgia said in surprise.

The whole village and the surrounding area used the Colemans' farm shop. Georgia's mum regularly went there and bought as many of their supplies as she could.

"Dan." Ben shot him a warning look.

"It's Georgia, Ben," Dan said, frowning at his brother. "We can tell her anything." He turned back to his friend, rifling through the paperwork on the table and pulling out a couple of letters. "There're fewer and fewer people coming through the doors," he explained. "Dad's out of his mind with worry." He showed Georgia a final demand for an unpaid vet's bill. "We just can't keep up with the bills if no one's buying from us."

"How long's this been going on?" Georgia asked.

Ben gave a hollow laugh. "Ever since that new supermarket opened in town."

"It's so much cheaper," Dan said with a rueful smile. "It's the sort of thing that's happening all over the place but we really thought we were safe here. Dad's gutted."

"We just need some way of marketing ourselves," Ben continued, looking thoughtful. "And no more setbacks!"

"Dan, I feel awful for not knowing," Georgia said. "Why didn't you say anything?"

Dan sighed. "We were hoping it would be a blip, that it was just that the supermarket was new," he said, placing the letters back under the pile on the table. "Still, let's just hope things improve soon. We surely can't be due any more bad luck!" He smiled properly at Georgia for the first time. "Let's talk about something else. This is too depressing. So, how were the trials? I need some good news, so tell me – yes, no? Did you make the team?"

Georgia grinned, in spite of how sorry she felt for Dan. "Yes," she said, the news finally sinking in.

Dan gave her a huge thumbs-up before slapping her on the back, grinning wildly.

"That's awesome, Georgia!" he said, sounding genuinely thrilled, and Georgia thought what a great friend he was, no matter what was going on in his life. "Bring on the Team Challenge!"

✰ ✰ ✰

For the rest of the afternoon, Georgia hung around on the farm, helping Dan unload boxes for the shop and bottle-feeding the three calves that lived in a stable adjacent to the yard. Their long eyelashes and dark curious eyes reminded Georgia of Lily and, for the hundredth time, she wondered what the palomino's foal would be like. She couldn't wait!

When Georgia cycled back up the drive to Redgrove stables to bring Lily in for the night, she was surprised to see Emma waiting for her, drumming her feet against the wall that she was sitting on. She jumped down when Georgia pulled up and fell into step beside her. "Hey, there," she said, sounding slightly awkward.

"Hey," Georgia said in response. "What are you doing here?"

She couldn't help but notice Emma's new jodhpurs and shiny black boots.

Emma picked up a lead rope and twirled it round in her hand, avoiding her friend's eyes. "You're not mad at me, are you?" she said finally, still looking at the ground.

Georgia trailed her foot in the mud and said nothing.

"I know I was with Lexie at the trials and I haven't been up here much," said Emma. "But what with Lexie offering me these riding lessons, and Dad saying I should take up her offer..." Her voice tailed off.

"It's all right, Em," Georgia sighed. "Just be careful, that's all."

"Careful?" Emma questioned. "What do you mean?"

"I'm not sure," Georgia shrugged. "It's just that I get a funny feeling about Lexie. Something's not quite right."

Emma looked defensive for a moment. "Lexie's absolutely fine, Georgia," she said coldly. "I've known her for ages. And she invited you over to the yard to see her ponies, didn't she?"

"I guess," Georgia shrugged, "although she hasn't exactly followed through on that."

"She will," said Emma. "She's just been busy."

The two girls talked for another few minutes or so, but it was horribly awkward and Emma excused herself at the first opportunity.

Georgia sighed heavily after her friend had left. She caught Lily and they walked back up to the yard, the mare's golden coat gleaming in the last rays of the sun. Georgia pulled on an ancient quilted jacket hanging in the tack room to ward off the evening's chill. The air was thick with the smell of a nearby bonfire as she led Lily into her stable and rugged her up. Georgia scratched behind her ears and Lily sighed contentedly, lowering her head and closing her eyes as she enjoyed the attention.

"Oh, Lily," Georgia said sadly. "Thank goodness for you." She thought back to a few weeks ago when Emma had excitedly announced that she wanted to start riding again and Melanie had given her lunge lessons. They had even spent

78

hours circling adverts in pony magazines as they laughed and daydreamed about Emma getting her own loan pony.

So much for that, Georgia thought. She hated being jealous but she couldn't help the feeling that kept flooding through her. She and Emma normally shared everything and had always been really close, but now that Emma was going to ride at Seven Birches and had a new friend in Lexie, they suddenly felt worlds apart...

CHAPTER TEN

"Hey, Georgia, do you fancy coming over to the yard on Wednesday after school?"

It was morning break a couple of days later, and Lexie had joined Georgia, Emma and Dan as they stood around in the playground, chatting. Emma must have said something to her, Georgia realised, feeling a warm glow that her friend had thought about her.

"You could meet River and look around the yard," Lexie went on without actually meeting Georgia's eyes. "Oh, and Dan – you can come too if you like," she said, casually, as if it were an afterthought.

"Thanks, Lexie," Georgia said, not knowing what else to say.

"Yeah, thanks," said Dan.

Lexie looked embarrassed and, gathering her bag, shot off to her next class.

To Georgia's surprise, Emma hung back instead of rushing off with her new friend. "You will come, won't you? You'll love it at the yard. It's so smart – like nothing you've ever seen before. Dad's just so happy I'm going to ride there instead of at Redgrove!"

Georgia felt a small bubble of annoyance forming. "So there's something wrong with Redgrove now, is there?" she blurted out. "You liked it well enough before!" And turning on her heel, she marched off down the corridor.

"Georgia!" Emma called after her.

But Georgia didn't turn back. Emma's dad was a snob. A horrible giant snob. And now it seemed that Emma was turning into one, too. She was getting a bit fed up with her going on about nothing else but Lexie and her amazing yard...

☆ ☆ ☆

"So what do you think, Dan?" said Georgia, as they pressed the buzzer to the heavy iron gates at Seven Birches on Wednesday evening. The gates swung back and the two of them walked their bikes up the drive.

"Well, it's certainly impressive." Dan let out a low whistle as they passed field upon field with outbuildings and arenas.

"It is, isn't it?" Georgia blinked. It was all she could do not to gape at what lay around her. A long sweeping drive flanked by neatly trimmed conifer bushes took them into the stable block, where the entrance was framed by an imposing archway, complete with tower clock. Roses clambered around the stone brickwork and even the yard floor itself had a mosaic of a leaping horse on the cobbles. There wasn't a wisp of hay or single shaving out of place.

Beyond the stable block lay the Olympic-sized arena set within a walled garden complex. Immaculate show jumps were in place, and far beyond that, Georgia could see the start of a mini cross-country course, which wound its way around the parkland.

"Wow!" she breathed.

"It's lush, isn't it!" Emma was suddenly beside Georgia, clad in a brand new bodywarmer with her hair in a neat ponytail. These days, she was looking more and more like the type of smart, horsey girl Georgia envied on rare trips to big events like Badminton.

"So, this is Herbie!" Emma walked Georgia and Dan into the yard and introduced them to a beautiful dun Connemara who was hanging his head over the stable door. He watched the visitors calmly before turning his attention back to his hay net. It was easy to see why Emma was so keen on riding here – the first pony they'd met was the most elegant equine specimen Georgia had ever seen, *apart from Lily*, she thought, forever loyal to her mare.

"Lexie's qualified him for Horse of the Year five years in a row," Emma said proudly, stroking his mushroom-coloured neck. "I either ride him, or Maggie, the grey, or even River sometimes."

"He's lovely, Emma," Georgia said.

"And he's perfect for Emma," a cool voice added.

Turning around, Georgia saw Lexie walk into the stable yard. She looked elegant as always in expensive chequered breeches that Georgia recognised from the local saddlery. She had picked them up herself and tried them on wistfully at least ten times.

Lexie's stepfather was with her and gave the group a curt nod. Lexie introduced them all, calling him Joe. Georgia and Dan shook his hand politely.

Joe paused as he grasped Dan's hand. "Coleman, you say?"

"Yes," Dan said, looking puzzled.

"Your dad owns the farm down the road?" Joe continued looking closely at Dan who was blushing.

"Yes, that's my dad's farm," he agreed, glancing at Georgia who shrugged.

"Down the road from Redgrove Stables." Joe

said this almost to himself, before he turned on his heel and clapped his hands. "Jason!" he barked as the whippet-thin man with the flat cap from the trials came scurrying over. "Make sure Lexie does her grid work tonight. I want River jumping perfectly, do you hear?"

Dan and Georgia hung around for a little longer, watching Emma ride Herbie in the indoor school. It was clear to see she was nervous. Jason was snappy and brusque in his style of teaching and Emma looked confused as she tried to follow his orders.

Herbie rolled his eyes and swished his tail, growing increasingly impatient as he was given the wrong aids. Georgia was almost certain that he was a highly bred Junior Grade A pony, which meant he'd won a certain amount of money competitively and would not be used to novice riders. She was amazed that Joe was letting Emma

ride him at all. She guessed it must be to show his
gratitude to Emma's dad for all the legal help he
was giving him.

Georgia felt an awful sense of disloyalty towards
her friend – but she knew that Emma just wasn't
an experienced enough rider for the Connemara.
She could barely watch as the pony put in a couple
of small bunny hops as Emma pushed him into
a clumsy canter, startling and unbalancing her.
Somehow she survived the rest of the lesson, but
she was white-lipped and clearly terrified … and
that wasn't a good start to anyone's riding career…

CHAPTER ELEVEN

"That was a bit weird, wasn't it?" Dan yelled over his shoulder later as he and Georgia biked their way back from Seven Birches in the growing dusk. "Lexie's stepdad knowing who I was, I mean."

"Yes, it was," Georgia shouted back. In fact, the whole set-up had seemed a little strange. She wasn't sure what to make of it, and worried for her best friend. Georgia had always trusted her instincts and there was something strange going on at Seven Birches that she couldn't quite put her finger on. Why was Lexie so keen for Emma to ride one of her best ponies when she was only a novice? And why had Joe taken such an interest in Dan?

As they rounded the corner to the Colemans' farm, Dan suddenly stopped in his tracks.

Parked in front of the bungalow was a sleek black estate car with tinted windows. It was far too shiny and clean to be any of Mr Coleman's friends. The farm collie, Hattie, sat sadly outside, but was soon whining for attention when she caught sight of Dan. She weaved in and out of his legs.

Dan pressed a finger to his lips and beckoned for Georgia to follow him into the porch where they could hear the muffled sound of a conversation inside. Mr Coleman's voice was distinct above the others and he sounded upset. There were at least two other men in the room.

"If you could just think about it overnight..."

It wasn't a local accent – London, maybe? And it was followed by what sounded like a fist being slammed down on the table.

"No!" Dan's dad's voice was firm but he was clearly upset. "No, no, NO! This farm has been in this family for five generations!"

Dan glanced at Georgia, his face a mixture of shock and worry. He opened the door to the kitchen, startling everyone inside. Dan's father was sitting at the table, looking small and grey in his old checked shirt. Usually so red-cheeked and cheery, he looked pale and anxious as he ran a hand through his sandy-coloured hair.

Two other men lounged in their chairs, one snapping a briefcase shut. Both had slick hair and shiny shoes, looking as out of place at the scrubbed wooden table as cats at Crufts. They both glanced uninterestedly at Georgia and Dan.

"Our offer still stands," one of them said to Mr Coleman, gesturing to his companion that it was time to leave. Standing up, he held out a hand to Dan's father, which wasn't accepted. Smirking, the man continued, "We'll see ourselves out then."

And with that, they were gone, purring down the farm drive in the black car, narrowly missing a cockerel who had strayed across their path.

"What's going on, Dad?" Dan demanded, sitting down next to his father.

Mr Coleman sighed and slumped his shoulders. "They're agents, Dan. Buyers for a large development company that wants our land to build on and then sell for a huge profit." He didn't seem to notice Georgia. He sounded angry now, his eyes flashing.

"What did you say?" Dan said, the colour

draining from his face.

"I said *over my dead body*!" Mr Coleman said loudly. "There's no way I'm letting this farm go. Not ever!"

"Well then, they can't do anything, can they?" Dan's voice was anxious.

His dad sighed, putting his head in his hands. "No, son, but somehow they've got hold of our accounts and know the shop's running at a loss." He glanced at the paperwork beside him. "I just don't know why we're losing customers. It's never happened before!" He looked bewildered and tired.

"It'll be all right, Dad." But Dan sounded unconvinced. "It's only a temporary thing – we'll start making money again soon."

His dad gave a wry smile and patted his son on the back. "I do hope you're right, Dan. We can't take any more setbacks."

Chapter Twelve

To Georgia's surprise, Emma invited her back to Seven Birches the following night to watch Lexie riding River. Cycling up the drive with her spaniel, Pip, running beside her, she felt a sense of unease. But at least there was no sign of Joe, or the fearsome Jason, just Lexie, schooling River around the walled arena.

Georgia watched with interest. Lexie was so light

and fluid, her hands soft and yielding, and River moved in total harmony with her. She looked so much more relaxed when she was by herself than when Jason was in the arena with her, barking instructions. There was a rare smile on her face as she leg yielded across the school, before cantering a perfect twenty-metre-circle. Georgia went to look for Emma and found her in a stable grooming Herbie.

"That was impressive," Georgia said, leaning in over the door. "Lexie's riding, I mean. She's a really good rider, isn't she?"

"Yeah, she is," Emma said, pulling a comb through Herbie's black mane. "When she's not jumping, that is... Jason and Joe, they..." She paused, busying herself with an imaginary knot in the mane.

"They what?" Georgia said curiously.

Emma looked thoughtful. "I dunno, Georgia.

It's just not the same as at Mel's, that's all. They make her jump when she doesn't want to. They're just pushy, I guess."

Georgia felt worried for Emma. "It's not making you lose your nerve, is it?"

"No … no," Emma said. "It's just that, well, sometimes I worry about Lexie."

"Is she scared?" Georgia thought back to when she'd watched Lexie jumping under her stepdad's watchful eye. But Lexie was such a natural in the saddle Georgia didn't know what she had to be afraid of.

"Not scared, exactly," said Emma. "Oh, I don't know. Forget I said anything. Anyway, the point is, she just can't say no to her stepdad."

"Why's her mum never about?" asked Georgia.

"She's always in London, shopping," said Emma.

"Oh," said Georgia. Poor Lexie. "It's weird her

stepdad knew who Dan was," she said, thinking back to last night.

"I guess everyone knows the farm shop," Emma replied, shrugging.

"Maybe," Georgia said, but she was unconvinced. She couldn't shake the strange feeling she had about Lexie's stepfather.

As Emma fumbled around with her gloves and hat, Lexie clattered into the yard. She said a brief hello to Georgia before tying up River and loosening his girths.

"Are you still up for jumping tonight, Emma?"

Emma looked startled. "What, without Jason here?" she said in a worried voice.

"It's better if he's *not* here," Lexie said coolly. "You can ride River."

"Em..." Georgia said and then stopped herself. She was about to say that, as a novice rider, she didn't think her friend was ready for River. But this was Lexie's yard and Emma rode here now. It wasn't her place to say anything.

Emma turned to Georgia. "Sorry, G, but would it be OK if you left? I get distracted with too many people watching."

"OK," Georgia said slowly, trying not to sound as hurt as she felt. She knew Emma wasn't up for jumping yet, and certainly not on a pony as feisty as River. She also knew she was only trying to impress Lexie. Georgia wanted to shake her and beg her to come back to Redgrove where Melanie would carry on teaching her on the kind and patient Wilson. River, although obedient, was a highly-strung and experienced pony.

Feeling dejected she picked up her bike and called for Pip, who was rustling in the conifers surrounding the yard.

"You know Mel would still be able to give you lessons if you wanted." Georgia blurted out the words before she could stop herself.

Emma looked momentarily guilty. "I know, Georgia, but this is where I ride now. Redgrove is fine but I want to learn to ride properly, and this is my chance to do that." But she didn't meet Georgia's eyes as she spoke and what she was saying sounded like a rehearsed speech.

"But Redgrove is perfect!" Georgia retorted, immediately defensive.

"What Emma means is that she can ride the best ponies here and learn properly, instead of always being fobbed off with a lunge lesson on an old plod," Lexie said, her words cutting into Georgia like a knife.

"But that's not how it is at all, is it, Em?" Georgia said, flushing. She turned to her friend. "Melanie's a good teacher. She was building you up slowly, and Wilson isn't a plod!"

Emma looked embarrassed. "I know that, G,"

she said quietly. "But I was only ever going to trot around the field with you at Redgrove. At least here I can actually ride and do stuff."

"But River's too much for you!"

Instantly, Georgia regretted her words. Emma turned towards her, eyes blazing. "Oh, you really think you're something, don't you!" she said harshly. "You get given a pony on loan, you get called up to trial for the Team Challenge, and now you dare to tell me what I can and can't do. Well, for your information, Lexie wouldn't let me ride her best pony if she thought he was too much for me!" Emma's normally pale complexion flushed pink and white in quick succession.

Georgia felt as though she had been slapped in the face. Jumping on her bike, she pedalled down the drive as fast as she could, her eyes streaming with tears. Maybe it was true that she did get all the attention at Redgrove. And Melanie did let her compete and ride her best pony, while loaning her Lily, but Emma had only got back into riding recently and Georgia knew it was important to build confidence up slowly. And Melanie had been looking into sorting out another horse for Emma.

Georgia gritted her teeth in frustration, trying to swallow her tears. Lexie had really got a hold over Emma and seemed determined to drive Georgia and her best friend apart!

CHAPTER THIRTEEN

Georgia spun up the driveway to Redgrove as quickly as she could to be greeted with a whicker of concern by Lily. Abandoning her bike on the yard, Georgia sprinted across the paddocks and flung her arms around the little palomino mare. Snuffling into her mane and sighing deeply, she felt instantly comforted. She decided to take Lily for a walk to clear her head. If nothing else, it would fill the time, but she was pretty sure it would make her feel better too. She didn't want to go home just yet – not when her mum would only question her reddened eyes and pale face.

Clinging to Lily's neck for support, with Pip bounding ahead, Georgia stumbled down the track towards the long meadow at the bottom of Redgrove. From there a meandering path took them along the edge of the woods bordering the Colemans' land.

Georgia was so engrossed in her thoughts that she was startled when Lily suddenly stopped and gave a nervous snort. Pip stopped as well, several yards ahead, her hackles rising as she gave a low growl.

"Come on, Lily," Georgia said, looking around. "There's nothing there."

Tugging on Lily's lead rope, she moved them forwards over the brow of the hill. Lily danced from side to side, her eyes fixated on the activity in the bottom valley.

Georgia squinted into the fading evening light. She'd been wrong; there *was* something there – she could see six or seven men in the valley, all in suits and all wearing wellies that looked as though they'd never seen a speck of mud before.

Hiding herself as best as she could, Georgia strained to hear what was going on. It looked like they were measuring the field, walking in a line with some sort of tape. One of the men was holding an official-looking clipboard. But this was the Colemans' land, Georgia was sure of it. What were they doing? She felt a growing sense of unease as one of the men glanced up in her direction. He shouted something that Georgia couldn't quite hear, and then the men hurried back to a couple of waiting cars. She felt sure she'd seen one of the cars before and then she remembered the sleek black saloon parked across the Colemans' farm drive.

Hurrying back to the yard as darkness enveloped them, she texted Dan with shaky hands, asking if he was at home.

✿ ✰ ✿

"No, no one told me anything about it," Mr Coleman said angrily. He was sitting at the kitchen table, the strain of recent events clearly evident on his face, the dark rings under his eyes proof that it was keeping him awake at night.

Dan was standing by the ancient Aga, mindlessly stirring something that smelled like it was burning. "It must have been those agents from the other day, measuring up," he said. His dad scowled and began sifting through the piles of letters on the table, as though he was going to find a solution among the paperwork.

Dan took hold of Georgia's arm and steered

her towards the living room. Their collie, Hattie yawned and blinked as she uncurled herself from the sofa. "We're in trouble, Georgia," he said, his voice low. He paused, absentmindedly stroking Hattie. "We've had an anonymous complaint – someone saying Dad doesn't look after his cows properly." The words caught in his throat.

"What?!" Georgia was startled. "But that's rubbish!"

"Of course it is." Dan put a finger to his lips and gestured towards the door. "But they've got a pretty good campaign going, and mud sticks. They're threatening to tell the papers. We think that's the reason no one's been coming to the shop. Reputation's everything and what with sales falling and the opening of the new supermarket, we don't stand a chance."

Georgia's heart sank. She couldn't understand it. Mr Coleman loved his golden Jersey cows just like she loved Lily. It was as if someone was deliberately trying to sabotage the Colemans' business. She couldn't think who, or why, but something was definitely going on ... she was sure of it...

✩ ✩ ✩

The headline in the local newspaper the next day confirmed their worst fears.

"Local farm shop guilty of malpractice," screamed the black letters above a picture of a forlorn looking black-and-white cow.

"Dad doesn't even have black-and-white cows," Dan said savagely, gathering up as many papers as he could and dropping them on the counter of the local newsagent. "Everyone knows ours are Jerseys."

Mr Spencer, the owner, cleared his throat, looking sympathetic. "I can't stop them putting out the papers, lad, I'm sorry," he said in his gruff voice.

"It's all right, Mr Spencer." Dan was still adding newspapers to the growing pile on the counter. "I'll buy all of these, if that's OK."

Mr Spencer began counting them. "Burn them, I would," he said, in a fierce voice. "You know we all support your dad, don't you?"

"Yeah," Dan said wearily, his shoulders slumping. "Tell that to all the other customers, though. It's only the village buying from us now, and that's not enough!"

Georgia thumbed through the pages. There was a big advert for the new supermarket in town and some sort of promotional bit about some development company Georgia didn't really understand. The picture showed a suited man shaking hands with the supermarket manager, and his sneery smile and slicked-back hair were instantly familiar. It was one of the agents who had visited the farm the other evening!

She showed the photo to Dan as he scrabbled in his pockets for money. He studied it too, making a face when he realised who it was. "Delta Developments," he said, frowning as he read the caption under the picture. "Well, I hope they never dare come back to our farm!"

CHAPTER FOURTEEN

Rain lashed down the sides of the horsebox as Melanie slowly manoeuvred her way through the narrow lanes. They were on there way to Janey's yard on Saturday morning for the Team Challenge training session. Georgia stared gloomily out of the window ahead, her knees tucked up to her chest. The wipers were on full power, squeaking noisily as they struggled to keep up with the deluge. It was not a good day for jumping. Thank goodness for Janey's indoor school and Mel's warm stables. Lily had been cosy in her stable with a brand new woollen rug and a full hay net when they had left.

Harry's horsebox was parked up by the school as they pulled into Janey's yard. His mum, head to toe in oilskins, rain dripping from her wide-brimmed hat, was scurrying around the lorry, getting Hector's tack together. Georgia caught sight of Harry sitting in the cab, feet on the dashboard, computer game on his lap, and a Jack Russell puppy curled up beside him.

"Yuck," Georgia said out loud as he smirked at her. He was just so spoilt!

A few minutes later, Georgia was warming up Wilson in the outdoor school, her long riding mac already drenched and heavy. She was concentrating so hard on getting the bay pony to go forwards against the driving wind that she nearly didn't notice the figure trotting a wobbly figure-of-eight next to her. The two horses almost collided as they changed rein. It was River.

"Watch out, Lexie!" Georgia cried.

Wilson came to an abrupt halt as the appaloosa pony spooked slightly to the side. The rider pulled back her hood. It was Emma.

"Em!" Georgia cried. "What are you doing here?"

Emma brought River to a standstill. She looked defensive, but scared, sitting rigidly in the saddle, her hands clenched tightly on the reins.

"Emma?" Georgia asked curiously. "Are you all right? What's going on?"

"Lexie's ill," Emma said, her voice barely carrying above the wind and rain. "She's in the horsebox, feeling sick. I said I'd warm River up."

Georgia opened her mouth and then closed it again. *Don't get involved*, she told herself firmly. It seemed like a crazy plan to her, but she'd learned by now that Emma was super-defensive when it came to her new friend.

☆ ☆ ☆

Training didn't go well that morning. Georgia couldn't concentrate on riding at all. She was worried about Dan's farm and Emma's inept experience on River had had a knock-on effect on her. Wilson was such a kind-hearted pony, but even he couldn't disguise Georgia's fumbling mistakes. She could barely bring herself to look at Melanie when they rode to the side.

She must be so disappointed, Georgia thought. *Sophie would never ride like this. I'm letting Wilson down.*

As Georgia knocked down yet another grid pole, Janey took her aside. "I don't think it's your day, Georgia," she said, her voice firm. "Why don't you get some more practice in at home first."

Georgia looked at Melanie, who nodded, her face slightly downcast. Georgia wanted to cry. Even worse, Emma only gave her a half-smile as she took River back to the horsebox with Lexie, who had finally appeared but not said a word all session.

✰ ✰ ✰

"It's only you that's right in my life now," Georgia said morosely as she rugged Lily up for the evening. They had just enjoyed a walk down to the bottom meadow where Georgia had sat on an upturned tree stump for what seemed like hours and told the little pony her worries.

It made Georgia feel better looking around her. It was the first place she and Lily had ridden together, before they knew the mare was in foal. She couldn't decide what she most looking forward to, riding Lily again or meeting Lily's newborn. She hoped the foal was palomino, just like her dam.

Leaning her cheek against Lily's neck, breathing in the unmistakable smell, Georgia felt tears pricking her eyes. Not only was she losing Emma's friendship, or at least that's what it felt like, but she had the upset of seeing Dan growing more and more withdrawn as the rumours continued to circulate about the farm. And just to put the icing on the cake, she couldn't ride properly and was letting Sophie and Wilson down. It was probably only going to be a matter of time before Janey replaced her. Georgia sighed.

"Oh, Lily," she said. "Whatever am I going to do?"

But Lily didn't have an answer for her. All she could do was gently nudge her owner as Georgia kissed her good night and then reluctantly let herself out of the palomino's stable.

✩ ✬ ✩

The Colemans' collie was still whining piteously

when Georgia reached the farm early the next morning, following a panicked phone call from Dan. The urgency and horror in his voice had frightened Georgia, so she had begged her mum for a lift to get there faster. Georgia's mum had taken one look at her daughter's pale freckled face, and agreed immediately.

"What's happened?" Georgia cried urgently as she jumped out of the car.

"First of all, poor Hattie cut herself on a barbed-wire fence early this morning," said Dan, pointing at the bandage on the collie's front right paw. He crouched in the entrance to the farm shop, hunched over his dog. "And that's not the half of it." His eyes were glassy with tears and he listlessly stroked Hattie who shivered and shivered beneath his hand.

"What else has happened?" Georgia said anxiously, looking in through the door to the farm shop. There was debris everywhere, shelves overturned, stock all over the place. Milk pooled on the floor. Mr Coleman was picking his way through the mess, flanked by Ben, who was shaking his head incredulously.

"We just found it like this," said Dan. "Someone must have broken in." He got to his feet and placed a comforting hand on his dad's shoulder. "It's so horrible, but it's going to be OK, Dad. That's what insurance is for."

Mr Coleman looked up as he tried to right the till, which had been thrown to the ground. The despair in his face was all too plain to see. He ran a hand through his curly hair. "But it's not going to be OK, Dan." His voice broke with emotion.

Dan lifted his head at the tone in his dad's voice. Mr Coleman sat down on one of the upturned milk churns that used to decorate the shop so cheerfully. "When the number of customers dropped and sales plummeted, the money stopped coming in but we still had costs to pay, overheads to meet, vet bills and the rest..." His voice trailed off. "I had to save money somewhere."

Dan looked sick. "You stopped paying the insurance?"

"Yes," said Mr Coleman, his head in his hands. "Don't you see?" he said, his voice cracking. "We're finished!"

☆ ☆ ☆

"So what will happen, Mum?" Georgia had been silent most of the way home until they had turned into the drive. They had helped the Colemans as best as they could, leaving them in the kitchen with mugs of tea once they had attempted to salvage as much of the farm-shop stock as possible.

Ben had been on the phone begging the insurance company to consider their previous payments and help them out, but they wouldn't budge.

Georgia had given Dan a big hug before she had left.

"I'll come and see Lily soon," he'd said, his voice quiet and sad. "I need a break from all this."

Georgia's mum switched off the ignition and turned to face her daughter. "I don't know, sweetheart," she said sadly. "When bad things happen to good people, it's just not right." She reached over and hugged Georgia, who clung to her for just a second. "Please come up to Redgrove with me, Mum," she said in a muffled voice.

"Of course." Mrs Black smiled. "I'm well overdue a visit to the expectant mother."

Chapter Fifteen

"So they've put a bid in." Dan was plaiting Lily's mane as he spoke. It was after school one evening a few days later. He had barely said anything all day, which made his words all the more significant.

Georgia looked up from where she was brushing out Lily's tail. "Who?" she asked, her heart sinking, knowing the answer. "Who's put in a bid?"

"The agents from that company, Delta Developments," Dan said bitterly. "They're like vultures, moving in for the kill." He patted Lily's neck. "There's no way Dad can refuse any offer now – the debts are too big, and the bank's hounding him to accept." He brushed away a tear as he spoke.

"But there must be something we can do," said Georgia, but she knew they were just easy words.

Dan shook his head. "I love that farm, Georgia. Mum loved it. Gramps loved it. Dad loves it. Ben was going to take it over and I was going to help him."

"Oh, Dan." Georgia's heart was breaking for him. But what exactly could she do or say to make it any better?

☆ ☆ ☆

"Emma?" Georgia hadn't spoken to her best friend properly for days now, other than small

talk at school. They had both pretended nothing was wrong, but the atmosphere between them was really strained. It was the longest they had gone without hanging out, and Georgia had felt nervous as she cycled to the neat cul-de-sac in the smart end of the village, where two shiny sports cars sat in the drive.

"Hey, Georgia." Emma was dressed for riding. "Dad's just about to drop me over to Lexie's." She hesitated, and then added, "I'm sorry about Dan. I heard what happened."

Georgia twisted her scarf in her fingers. "Yeah, it's pretty bad," she admitted. Then, trying to be cheerful, she asked, "Are you still enjoying riding at Seven Birches?"

Emma looked up. She seemed a little surprised by the question. "Yes, yes, I guess," she said. Her voice wavered only slightly, but Georgia picked up on it immediately.

"Emma?"

"Don't," Emma said crossly. "I know you want me to come back to Redgrove but I wouldn't have a pony like Herbie or River to ride there. OK, so sometimes it's tough but..." She glanced behind her. "Anyway, that's where Dad says I have to stay."

"Your dad?" said Georgia. "But why?"

But Emma didn't have a chance to answer as, at that moment, her father appeared, dressed as always in his grey pinstripe suit. He was talking into his mobile, in a hushed, lowered tone. "Listen," he was saying, his voice quiet but angry. "This wasn't what I advised..." Seeing the girls' faces, he snapped the phone shut, smiling brightly. "Hello, Georgia," he said, before turning to his daughter. "Ready to go riding, Emma?" he asked, sounding falsely cheerful.

"Sure am, Dad," said Emma. "Are you staying

to see Joe at the yard after dropping me?"

Her dad's face clouded. "No," he said. "Not this time. I've got some other business to attend to."

Shrugging at Georgia, Emma climbed into the car. "See you at the Champs," she said.

"But I—" Georgia opened her mouth to speak but Emma had already shut the passenger door. She stared after the car as it pulled away. She hadn't had a chance to talk to her friend properly about any of the things going on at the moment. Every time she tried to, something else seemed to get in the way. Letting out a heavy sigh, Georgia wheeled her bike back down the road.

☆ ☆ ☆

"So how about this trip to Wales, then?" Melanie asked.

The mood around the kitchen table at Redgrove Farm was sombre as Georgia sat down that evening. Sophie was back for the weekend and was sitting on the scrubbed wooden table, her hair a riot of blue and pink streaks. Her feet were clad in trendy sheepskin boots, kicking the air as she listened to the latest dramas in the village.

"Come on, Georgia," said Sophie. "Let's go and see Wilson before it gets dark."

"Sure thing." Georgia had felt slightly shy when she first saw Sophie but the older girl grabbed her hand now and they raced down to the stables.

"Wilson! Wilson!" Sophie cried, flinging her arms around her horse and burying her nose into his mane. The bay pony whickered in delight at seeing his young mistress. "He looks really well, Georgia." She grinned. "And how are the Team Challenge practices going for the Autumn Champs?"

Georgia made a face. "Not great," she said truthfully. "I'm letting Wilson down with my riding."

"What are you talking about?" Sophie said, nudging her shoulder. "You're the best rider I know!"

"That's not exactly true," Georgia said, but she blushed in pleasure at the compliment. Sophie tucked her arm in hers as Georgia told her about the last team practice and they wandered round to the next stable to greet Lily, who bustled over with Callie by her side.

Sophie kept listening closely as she stroked Lily's golden neck. "Listen," she said once Georgia had stopped speaking, "we all go through these stages. I believe in you. Mum believes in you, or she'd never let you ride Wilson. And just think of the future you and Lily are going to have." She smiled warmly. "Next time that I'm home for a few days, why don't I give you some lessons, just you and me?" She paused, thoughtful. "Sometimes Georgia, you have to let go of any worries and just ride. I'm sure the problem is that you're over-thinking things."

Georgia grinned at her friend gratefully. "You could be right. And thanks, Sophie. That would be amazing!"

"And in the meantime, I think it's time you had a change of scene, don't you?" said Sophie. "Come on. Let's go and tell Mum to plan that trip to Wales."

Melanie tried and failed to look cross as the girls bounced noisily back into the kitchen, talking at the tops of their voices.

"When are you going to take Georgia to Wales, Mum?" Sophie asked.

Her mother smiled. "What about next weekend? Georgia – what do you say?"

Georgia nodded gratefully. Sophie was right. A break was exactly what she needed.

CHAPTER SIXTEEN

True to her word, the following Sunday Melanie drove the four-by-four up the motorway towards the Severn bridge with Georgia in the front seat. Georgia remembered her last journey up to Wales in the school coach, before she had the chance encounter with Lily on the mountainside.

"What have you got there?" Melanie asked her.

"Photos," said Georgia, clutching a handful of

photographs ready to show Eric Williams, Lily's breeder.

Melanie smiled. "That's nice," she said.

Lily had been Eric's star pony before he'd retired. He'd expected great things from her, but that was before his granddaughter, Jemma, had got hold of her and ruined her by treating her cruelly. It would be lovely to show him how Lily was getting on – and share her secret with him. Lily held a special place in Eric's heart.

Finally, after driving over miles of twisty mountain roads, they reached Eric's small cottage on the side of a hill just outside a small mining village. Georgia was pleased to be getting away from Redgrove, but she hadn't been that keen to leave Dan. Now that the agent had put in an official bid to Dan's dad, it looked more likely than ever that he would have to sell the farm.

Eric was leaning on his stick in the doorway as

the car pulled up to the cottage, a yellow Labrador by his feet. Any fears Georgia had about coming to Wales vanished when he gave her the widest smile she had ever seen. Georgia remembered how much Lily had adored her former owner.

"Come in, come in." Eric beckoned them into the cottage where the warmth was welcome relief from the October chill. The small, cosy kitchen was covered in old photos of ponies in the show ring, rosettes and sashes, most of them bearing the words "supreme champion". Georgia was immediately drawn to a photo that took pride of place on the sideboard, a gorgeous palomino mare and a tiny champagne-coloured foal. Georgia knew straight away it was Lily, whose coat had darkened slightly with age. The huge eyes and the small neat head gave her away even at such a young age. "Magical," she breathed.

After two cups of tea and a lot of catching up, Georgia produced her own photos of Lily. One was from before they knew she was in foal and showed Georgia astride her in the long meadow band, and another showed her rugged up in her stable with Callie next to her.

"So she's pregnant, you say?" Eric gazed and gazed at the photos in silence before balling his thumbs into the corner of his eyes. When he could finally speak, his voice was thick with emotion. "She really was my favourite," he whispered. "I'm so glad she's with you."

"We love her," Georgia said simply.

They smiled at each other – an understanding passing between them, young and old.

Melanie cleared her throat. "Is everything OK here, Mr Williams? I mean, with your family."

Eric gave a rueful smile. "Well, after all the unfortunate goings-on with Lily, Jemma did a month in a young offenders' institution," he said sadly. "Her mother's still running the stud, but once word got out, you know –" His voice tailed off and he gazed at the photos on his lap again, no doubt thinking back to the glory days of Carlamu, when he was a strong young man.

Suddenly, with a speed that defied his age, he was on his feet, his dog barking in excitement. "Anyway," he cried, clapping his hands together. "My girl's in foal! There's only one stallion around here and he's a real champ. I think you'll be pleased. Do you have walking boots?"

✿ ✿ ✿

Tripping and stumbling over the rough grass, Melanie and Georgia followed Eric and his dog as he limped ahead with his stick. Finally they reached the top paddocks surrounding Carlamu, the beautiful cobbled yard a jewel in the valley below them. Eric leaned on his stick and gave a long low whistle.

Georgia held her breath as the sound carried over the fields, causing all of the ponies to lift their heads in unison and prick their ears. Then a muscular red roan whinnied and pawed the ground before thundering towards them, and Georgia knew in an instant it was him.

"Easy boy, easy, easy," Eric crooned as the roan slid to a stop next to him, whickering gently and snuffling at his hands.

"Carlamu Rowan," Eric said proudly, rubbing his hand down the pony's face.

"Wow…" Melanie and Georgia spoke in unison.

Rowan was confirmation-perfect, so handsome and strong but with the kindest eyes. "This is your stallion," Eric continued as Rowan stood quietly next to him. "I bred Rowan eight years ago, from another line to Lily," he explained. "With Lily's heritage and Rowan as the sire, your foal can't be anything but a champion!"

☆ ☆ ☆

As Melanie and Georgia climbed into the four-by-four to leave, Georgia turned to Eric. "Thank you," she whispered. "Thank you for letting us come, but more importantly, thank you for letting us keep her."

Eric smiled. "She's special, that girl." He leaned against his stick. "I wouldn't have it any other way. Still, I can sense things aren't right for you at the moment. Are there troubles at home?"

Georgia nodded, taken aback that he could be so perceptive. She hadn't mentioned anything about Dan or her falling out with Emma.

"Well, mark my words," Eric continued. "Everything will come good. Lily came into your life for a reason. She'll bring the answers, you'll see."

"Do you really think so?" asked Georgia.

"Think so?" said Eric. "I know so. Goodbye Georgia. Melanie." He smiled and closed the door, tapping the roof of the car as they drove off, leaving Georgia completely speechless.

CHAPTER SEVENTEEN

The next few weeks passed in a blur. Sophie was as good as her word, and on a break from university, she had taken time to coach Georgia patiently in the bottom field.

"You can do it, G," she said, encouragingly, as Georgia trotted round in a perfect circle on Wilson. "You just have to forget about everything else when you ride."

It was true, Georgia knew. As she and Wilson flew around the Working Hunter course they'd set up in the growing dusk, riding felt better than it had for ages.

She'd been able to carry this confidence to the team practices and now, here she was, the morning of the Autumn Championships with the Team Challenge ahead of her. Georgia groaned as she rolled over and turned off her alarm clock. She opened one bleary eye. 4.30 a.m. It was so early! But she had to get up to make sure everything was ready.

Georgia pulled the duvet back over her head just for a moment. It was raining again, and her window rattled as the wind whistled in and out of the small gap in the frame. It sounded most uninviting!

When Georgia eventually emerged downstairs, her mum was up as well, already dressed in jeans and a jumper, feeding Pip a bit of toast at the kitchen table and nursing a coffee. Her mum had desperately wanted to come along and support her, but an important client had asked for a meeting to discuss a new commission and he was only in the vicinity for one day. Mrs Black had wanted to postpone the meeting but Georgia had convinced her not to. She knew she had her mum's unwaivering support and they couldn't afford to miss out on potential customers for her mother's paintings.

"All right, sweetheart?" Mrs Black said, glancing in concern at her daughter, who was looking smaller and paler than ever. Georgia nodded, her stomach flipping over with nerves.

They drove the short distance to Redgrove Farm in silence, Georgia feeling sicker and sicker. To her astonished delight, Dan was waiting for her outside Lily's stable.

"Dan!" she gasped, once her mum had given her a final good-luck hug and she'd jumped out of the car.

"Hey, Georgia." He managed a weak smile.

"What are you doing here?" she asked him. "Not that I'm not pleased to see you, of course!"

"I wanted to come and support you, of course," said Dan.

Georgia was so touched, she couldn't speak. Instead, she threw her arms around him in gratitude. He clung to her for just a few seconds, and Georgia felt him trembling.

"Delta Developments are taking over the farm tomorrow," he whispered into her shoulder.

"Tomorrow!" Georgia gasped. She pulled back and looked into his face. She knew that it had been on the cards but she hadn't expected it to happen so quickly.

"Yes," Dan nodded. "Dad's fighting to the bitter

end but there's really nothing he can do now."

There was a pause. Georgia didn't say anything but gave Dan another long hug.

"Now then," he said eventually, drawing back and giving Georgia the full benefit of his smile. "Haven't you got a championship to win?"

☆ ☆ ☆

As Melanie loaded Wilson into the lorry, Georgia heard a little whicker coming from the stable that Callie and Lily shared. The two horses were watching the preparation for the show with interest. Georgia stroked Lily's nose. There was something different about her, but she couldn't quite put her finger on it.

"Mel?" she called anxiously.

Melanie came over and looked at the little palomino mare. Her tummy had certainly got a lot larger in the last couple of weeks, and her udder had also started to enlarge, but according to the vet's calculations, she wasn't due for at least two weeks.

Patting Lily, Melanie let herself into the stable and took a closer look. "She's fine, Georgia. She looks nice and relaxed. I'd say she was still a way off."

"But Simon will keep an eye on her today, won't he?" Georgia was twiddling her fingers anxiously. She hated to leave her pony, even if it was for an important competition.

Melanie smiled. "Of course," she said, nodding in the direction of her husband, who they could see through the kitchen window frying bacon and eggs and chatting to the terriers at the same time. "She's in good hands. Although I think we'd better leave Callie and Lily in the stable today. What do you reckon?"

Georgia looked at the sky. The earlier storm was passing, but the morning was still pitch black. It was going to be a wet, stormy day, of that she was sure. She nodded, giving Lily a final hug. "I think that's a really good idea!"

☆ ✿ ☆

It was a long journey to the championships. Dan fell asleep almost immediately but Georgia was too nervous, sitting bolt upright. Her phone bleeped and she pulled it out. It was from Sophie.

Remember what I told you the text read. *We all believe in you – Lily most of all! Ride for her and like nothing else matters.*

Georgia felt a little warm feeling in the pit of her stomach and her confidence grew, just a little. One thing was for sure. She was going to do her very best.

☆ ✿ ☆

The Show Pony Autumn Championships were being held at a prestigious venue that was often used for international dressage competitions.

Flags from countries all over the world lined the long drive, which was accessed by electric gates. A security guard sitting in a booth buzzed them in as they arrived, smiling through the open window.

"Good luck today!" he called.

Dan and Melanie grinned and thanked him. Georgia just nodded mutely. She had the distinct feeling that if she opened her mouth she might be sick!

Harry's box was already in the lorry park ahead of them. Lexie's, the familiar DD logo on the side, was next to it. The area was quickly filling up with huge horse boxes, trailers and shiny four-by-fours. Friends and family of the competitors milled around under golf umbrellas, drinking coffee from paper cups and chatting excitedly. As they parked up next to Harry, Georgia was amused to see him leap out from the cab, green to the gills and pressing his hand to his mouth. So he did get nervous after all!

The Fishers' trailer soon pulled in and Lottie, as smiley as ever, gave Georgia a wave and a "I'm-so-nervous" grimace, which just made Georgia feel even more terrified. Now the team had all arrived, although she hadn't actually laid eyes on Lexie yet.

So where was she?

Settling Wilson into his day stable, Georgia was just lugging his hay net from the box when she collided with a panicky figure running in the opposite direction. It was Emma, her face pale and her hair a tangled mess.

"Emma?" cried Georgia. "Whatever's the matter?"

Emma was panting hard. "It's Lexie!" she gasped, and leaned against the side of the box to steady herself. "She's disappeared!"

CHAPTER EIGHTEEN

"Disappeared? What on earth do you mean?" Melanie guided Emma into the living area of the horsebox. "Sit down," she ordered, as Dan poured her a tea from the thermos mug and Georgia gave her a blanket to put round her shoulders. "And then you can tell us everything."

Emma accepted it gratefully. Her clothes were dripping wet and she looked freezing cold.

"Well…" She took a deep breath. "We got here really early. I helped Lexie stable River and she said she was just going to get a drink, but that was over half an hour ago. No one has seen her since!"

"Who are you with today?" Melanie asked, getting things straight in her mind.

"Just Jason," Emma said. "Lexie's stepdad isn't here. He's got some business to attend to or something. Lexie told him she doesn't want to ride any more, but Joe won't accept it and has been pushing and pushing her and now she's just had enough! Georgia, I'm really scared she's done something stupid!"

Georgia reached over and squeezed her friend's hand.

"Don't be silly." Melanie was on her feet now, thinking fast. "She's frightened of jumping, that's all. It's been coming for a while."

"What do you mean?" said Emma.

"You must have noticed how terrified she looked at practices," Melanie replied. "It was blindingly obvious."

So I was right, Georgia thought to herself. *Why didn't I just say something?*

"Does she have a mobile?" Melanie continued.

"Yes," Emma said, fishing her own phone from her pocket. "I've tried to ring her at least twenty times – it just goes straight to answerphone."

Dan suddenly spoke up. "What about the team?"

Melanie looked grim. "We need four riders – we can't compete without the fourth. We'll be eliminated." She looked sadly at Georgia. "And you guys have worked so hard."

"She was like this when she was younger," Emma said, typing furiously into her phone as she spoke. "When her mum and dad split up. She used to just take off back then too!"

When they went to find Janey and the rest of the team in the temporary stable area, Georgia noticed that River looked skittish and unsettled in comparison to Wilson, who was munching on his hay net, and Hector, who was snoring on the floor, oblivious.

Melanie had quickly filled everyone in on the situation and Janey was now deep in discussion with a bowler-hatted steward. Harry paced up and down angrily, waiting for the verdict, and Lottie sat slumped on a hay bale, clearly devastated. Emma perched herself next to Georgia and immediately began trying her phone again, her face pale with worry.

Although Georgia felt absolutely crushed at the prospect of going home without competing, at the moment she was more concerned about Emma, who seemed to be somehow blaming herself.

"You just have to be a four, madam." The

steward's voice broke into her thoughts. "It's the rules and there is nothing I can do about it."

"Well, that's it, then." Harry immediately started to toss things into a trunk that stood outside Hector's stable. "It's all over."

Lottie started sobbing quietly and Georgia's heart sank.

Suddenly, Emma leaped up from the hay bale. "It's Lexie!" she cried. "She's texted back!"

"And what does she have to say for herself?" Janey asked impatiently, turning away from the steward.

"Um, she says she's sorry and that she's back in the lorry now, getting changed." Emma scrolled down the message, gazing intently at the screen. "She says she'll meet you all in the ring!"

Georgia's heart leapt and Harry let out a whoop.

"Right," said Janey, beaming, "there's no time to lose. Let's get tacked up and warmed up."

As everyone starting rushing around, Georgia noticed Jason come into the stable block with River's bridle and saddle. He declined Emma's offer of help and she stood for a moment looking uncomfortable and out of place. As Georgia buckled up Wilson's girth, she tried to catch her friend's eye.

Emma didn't look at her directly but mumbled, "I'll just go and see Lexie," and hurried off in the direction of the trailer.

Georgia shook her head. Something wasn't quite adding up with all this but there was no time to think about it now. Promising herself that she would talk to Emma properly at the first opportunity, she turned her mind to the competition.

The team had already wasted precious time. The four needed to jump in their allocated order, which meant Lexie would jump last – and Georgia just hoped she would be ready and wouldn't bottle it again. Although the fences were not as high as they had been jumping in practice, the course was technical, and Georgia knew that the pressure of a crowd watching would make things much, much harder.

She forgot about her own nerves and started to worry about Lexie instead. Jason had tacked River up, scowling. He clearly didn't think much of Lexie's behaviour and he was also probably worried about what his boss would say when he found out that Lexie had nearly thrown the competition. Still, Georgia couldn't think about that now. They were all walking over to the ring and she needed to focus.

The class consisted of seven jumps, and then a short individual section where the competitors had to demonstrate their pony's paces, including a gallop on the long side. Lottie was first in the ring.

The rain had picked up again, and both Lottie and her pony squinted into the deluge as her mum removed the rug from the pony's quarters.

"Good luck," Janey said, patting Lottie's pony's neck. "You can do this!"

Georgia was trying to concentrate on keeping Wilson calm and collected against the howling wind and rain in the warm-up arena as she watched Lottie go in. She noticed that Lexie still hadn't come out of her trailer and River was tossing his head and pawing at the ground, dancing from side to side, as Jason tried to hold him steady. River being spooked wasn't going to be a good start for Lexie.

"Georgia!" A shrill cry interrupted her thoughts. It was Janey, striding out of the arena, clad in a wax jacket and hat. "Five minutes, Georgia," she called, holding up her hand. "Harry's going in now."

Lottie was walking behind her on a long rein.

She had a look of relief on her face that meant she must have done well.

"Clear!" She grinned at Georgia, giving her a thumbs-up sign.

"You'd better make your way down to the entrance, Georgia." Janey was consulting a programme. "You don't want to miss your time!"

Her spirits lifted a little by Lottie's result, Georgia tried to push away concerns about Lexie and focus on the task in hand. The minutes were flying by and Harry was about to enter the arena.

"Good luck," Georgia called.

Harry turned to her and grinned, but his face was pale.

He's actually really nervous! Georgia thought. For the first time, she felt a smidgen of empathy towards him. She watched as he nudged Hector into the ring and the gates closed behind him. Melanie had thrown a rug over Wilson's hindquarters to keep him warm and she felt him beneath her as solid and collected as ever. Georgia couldn't tell now if it was nerves or the cold that was causing her teeth to chatter. She patted the dependable bay on the neck, hoping some of his confidence would rub off on her.

Harry jumped clear, like he always did. Hector wasn't the flashiest horse on the showground, but what he lacked in dazzle, he more than made up for in personality and talent as his long powerful legs pushed him into a crowd-pleasing gallop, feathers flying.

Harry leaned over from Hector to pat Georgia on the back as he left the arena. It was her turn next.

Melanie placed her hand on Georgia's boot and squeezed her leg. "Just remember, G, whatever happens, we're proud of you," she said, smiling up at her.

Georgia swallowed, a lump forming in her throat. Dan was on the other side of her, his arm slung over Wilson's neck. She was so lucky to have their support, no matter how she did. She took a deep breath. Now, for the next five minutes, nothing mattered. Not the farm, or the troubles with Lexie. It was just her and Wilson, and the competition course.

CHAPTER NINETEEN

There was silence as Georgia entered the arena. The stadium seats were completely full – the Show Pony Autumn Championships was a huge date on the equine calendar. Wilson spooked slightly at the elaborate floral displays decorating the jumps, before Georgia nudged him into his trademark rolling canter.

There were only seven jumps. She reminded

herself that they'd done far more at home, but even so, her stomach was flipping and spinning with the pressure.

"Easy, Wilson," she crooned. "Easy does it."

The bowler-hatted judge nodded to her, and her round began.

Over the first, an upright gate, and straight into a double. Wilson sailed over the brush, and easily over the planks, which had already seen a number of refusals, before turning the sharp corner into the dreaded water splash – the same jump Georgia had fallen at during the team selection.

"Go on, boy," she whispered to Wilson, who flicked an ear back in response. She knew she had to ride strongly into the fence and not hesitate.

She nudged him forwards, sitting quietly, moving as one with him. Over another gate and down towards another double, and over a single brush before cantering down towards the last jump, an imposing mock stonewall.

Georgia half-halted Wilson before turning the final corner, giving him a tiny scratch on his withers. It was nearly over. They flew over the wall like it was a stick on the ground and Georgia was half-crying and half-cheering as the arena burst into applause.

The hardest bit over, she really enjoyed herself during her individual show, putting Wilson into a striking medium trot across the diagonal and really going for it in their gallop as the bay pony flew around the arena, his long strides eating up the ground.

"Amazing, amazing!" Melanie could hardly contain her excitement as Georgia trotted out of the arena.

"You were brilliant, Wilson!" Georgia dropped down on to the bay's neck to give him a massive hug, and Melanie slung a rug over his hindquarters to keep off the rain. She passed Georgia a jacket.

"You couldn't have done any better, G!" she said. "I'm so *so* proud of you!"

At that moment Lexie rode into the ring, her body stiff and her hands clenched tightly on River's reins. Georgia threw her an encouraging smile, but her riding hat was pushed down so far over her eyes, it was impossible to see her face.

River cantered forward hesitantly. His stride was choppy and he didn't seem to be responding to Lexie as he usually did. The bowler-hatted steward nodded and Lexie rode towards the first fence. Her posture was stiff and she was obviously giving River mixed signals, something Georgia had never seen her do before. She'd always ridden so naturally despite her fear.

Georgia gasped. Something was really wrong! River was approaching the jump too quickly, then he skittered and veered sharply away at the last minute, dropping his shoulder and throwing Lexie to the ground, where she hit the soft sand arena with an audible thump.

The crowd gasped as the rider lay quite still on her back. The brim of her hat had tilted up and, in the split second before she pulled it down again, Georgia saw that it wasn't Lexie at all – it was Emma!

She jumped off Wilson, threw his reins at Melanie and ran into the arena.

"Emma!" she cried as her friend groaned and got groggily to her feet.

Someone had caught River and was leading him back towards her.

"I'm afraid that's elimination for you, Lexie," the judge was saying in a kindly voice, unaware that it wasn't Lexie at all. "Do you want to hop back on?"

Emma shook her head, her bottom lip bleeding where she had bitten it from the fall. She was crying.

"Emma, don't worry!" Georgia had her arm around her friend as she led her out of the ring. "Are you OK? What were you thinking, taking Lexie's place?"

Emma lifted her tear-stained face and looked at Georgia. "You all seemed so disappointed that the team couldn't compete so I thought I'd take her place. I knew she'd left her competition clothes in the trailer and as I've ridden River before, I thought I'd give it a go..." Emma paused to let out a shuddering sob and Georgia tried to hug her. But Emma was shaking her head now and backing away. "Something's happened, Georgia. Lexie's found something out," Emma mumbled. "I'm sorry – I'll explain later. I've got to go."

And without a backward glance, she slipped

past the steward and ran out into the rain.

✩ ✪ ✩

Georgia stood rooted to the spot, speechless, thoughts crowding in on her. She had to talk to the rest of the team about what had just happened and to Melanie and Dan. What Emma had done was incredibly brave, but stupid too. Anything could have happened – she could have hurt herself badly or River could have been injured.

And what was Lexie's part in all this? Was making Emma practise on River, bringing her along to the show and then disappearing, leaving her competition clothes in the trailer, part of some plan? And what was it that she'd found out?

Another steward came racing over.

"Mounted presentation, please!" he called in a clipped voice. "Back to the main arena!"

Emma had already left, and Jason had hurried out of the arena with River, his face like thunder, obviously anticipating what his boss would say about a novice riding one of his precious horses in a show.

Georgia heard Janey talking to the steward in her usual brusque way. "One of our riders was disqualified. I doubt we're needed at the award ceremony."

"What's the name?" asked the steward, looking down his list.

"Round Barrow," replied Janey.

"Round Barrow..." The steward consulted his clipboard. "Believe it or not, you're actually on the prize list. Please make your way to the main arena now!"

"Really?" said Georgia. She turned to meet the incredulous gazes of Harry and Lottie. All three of them had jumped a clear round, but it seemed incredible that they were placed when one of their team had been eliminated.

Hardly believing their luck, none of them spoke as they had a frantic five minutes of re-tacking and adjusting their clothes. When they were all ready, they clattered back down towards the international arena, where the other teams were just starting to parade.

Melanie ran alongside Georgia, just as they entered the ring. She was waving a copy of the rule book. "It says here that as long as all four started, even if someone is eliminated or falls, you can still make it through. We had three clear rounds, after all, so you never know!"

Georgia let out a low whistle. "That would be amazing," she whispered.

CHAPTER TWENTY

The atmosphere in the stadium was electric as the Round Barrow team walked their mounts forward. The three ponies pricked their ears in anticipation and seemed to grow at least two hands, striding out in perfect sync.

The three team mates grinned at one another, and Georgia determined to set aside her worries about Emma and Lexie for the moment. The stewards directed the teams to line up against the long side of the arena. Some of the ponies were fidgeting and even rearing slightly on the spot but Hector, Wilson and Songbird were all calmly standing stock still.

The couple who were going to present the prizes to the teams placed in the top three were wearing black tie and a fancy sparkly evening dress. It was a funny sight on a wet afternoon at an equestrian centre. It all added to her growing feeling of excitement – maybe they had been placed in the team challenge after all!

At last the positions were called out. The tannoy announced the teams in reverse order from ninth, and with each announcement came a small cheer from the stadium and the presentations of the rosettes to the happy team members. Georgia couldn't believe it when they got to fourth place and they still hadn't been called.

Fourth place went to a neighbouring pony club.

They had! They'd been placed! Now it was just a question of where…

"And bronze goes to Edgeworth Hunt!"

Cheers erupted from the arena.

Georgia held her breath.

"The silver winners of the Working Hunter Team Challenge … Round Barrow Pony Club!" The words came out loud and clear over the speaker.

Melanie and Janey both cheered loudly as all three members threw their arms around their ponies' necks. Their excitement was so all-consuming that they barely heard the announcement for first place, which went to a team that had secured four clear rounds.

The lap of honour for the teams placed in the top three was the most exciting thing Georgia had ever done. The man in black tie and the lady in the sparkly dress had presented them with huge silver and white rosettes and a sash. They followed the winning team in the canter around the arena as loud pop music blasted out, and the crowds cheered.

Georgia and Lottie grinned at each other and rolled their eyes in mock disgust at the music. But it was a moment Georgia would never forget. She only wished Emma was there too. She had asked the steward if she could take a rosette for her and he had kindly given her one. She patted the pocket of her jacket where she had folded it safely. Emma deserved it, just for her brave attempt. What she had done was reckless, but luckily no harm was done. And she had done it out of friendship. Without her, Round Barrow would never have been able to compete, let alone win silver!

Melanie glanced anxiously at the sky as they loaded Wilson to start the journey home. It hadn't stopped raining all day and the lorry park was almost a river as weary ponies and jockeys trudged back to their respective boxes. Wilson was already wearing two rugs but was only too eager to hurry up the ramp into the dry of the box.

"I just hope we don't meet any flooded roads," Melanie said anxiously, turning the key in the ignition. "You OK, Dan?" she asked, as he huddled in the passenger seat next to Georgia. He turned to Melanie and smiled weakly, unable to speak. Georgia took his hand in hers and squeezed it. She knew that when he returned to the farm he was going to have to face up to the fact of his home being sold and the reality was clearly just starting to hit him.

The journey home was long, under dark and threatening skies. None of the passengers spoke – each of them was lost in their own thoughts. The motorway was busier than normal and Melanie had to crawl along slowly in the inside lane in a never-ending trail of headlights. Eventually, the silence was interrupted as Georgia's mobile phone rang loudly, making them all jump.

"It's Sophie," Georgia said, frowning at the screen. She pressed answer. "Hello?"

"Oh, Georgia, thank goodness!" Sophie's voice was ragged. Panic instantly rose in Georgia's throat as the older girl spoke. "Are you nearly back?"

"In about half an hour, I reckon. Sophie – what's wrong?" Georgia struggled to keep her voice calm.

"It's the river!" Sophie's voice rose at least two octaves. "It's burst its banks, the stables are about to flood, and Georgia…"

"Yes…" Georgia's heart was in her mouth.

"I think Lily has gone into labour!"

☆ ☆ ☆

Never had a journey gone so slowly. As Melanie

carefully inched the horsebox back to Redgrove Farm, the damage the storm had caused became more and more apparent. There was debris everywhere – fallen branches and tiles missing from roofs, and the fields shimmered under deep water where river after river had burst their banks.

Dan was still gripping Georgia's hand as, at last, they drove up Redgrove's long drive.

"Quick!" Melanie urged Georgia, but there was no need – she was already jumping out of the door as they pulled into the yard. The bottom meadow was a raging torrent and the floodwater lapped the edge of the cobbles.

Simon was in the yard in an overcoat and wellies. His usually sunny face was taut with worry as he carried sandbags to place at the edge of the stables in an attempt to keep the water at bay.

"Lily!" Georgia raced over to the palomino who was pacing her stable. She whinnied when she caught sight of Georgia and Callie gave a shrill cry, picking up on the vibes in the yard.

As Melanie unloaded Wilson, she took off his travelling boots and put him into the third stable.

"How bad is it?" She turned to Simon, her voice low.

Simon ran a worried hand through his hair. "It's bad," he said. "Really bad…"

Chapter Twenty-One

"Oh Lily, Lily," Georgia cried into the mare's mane. She felt a wave of guilt flood through her. She never should have left her, and wished she had trusted her instinct that morning when she noticed something different about her pony. No amount of glory or rosettes came close to the love she had for the little palomino.

"It's going to be OK," Melanie reassured her,

putting her hand on Georgia's arm. "But she is foaling early, Georgia." She glanced anxiously outside at the rising floodwater and silently said a small prayer. They had a long night ahead.

Simon was pacing the perimeter of the yard as they stepped out of the stable.

"Melanie!" he called, the concern unmistakable in his voice.

The floodwater had now reached the edge of Wilson's stable, and he watched in alarm as the water started to lap under the door.

"We're going to have to get them out," Simon said decisively.

Georgia, Melanie and Dan all turned to him. They knew he was right. The yard was going to flood in a matter of minutes, and with Lily going into labour, it was hard to imagine a worse scenario!

"But how?" asked Georgia. "We don't have

enough horse boxes."

Normally so calm and methodical, even Melanie looked panicked as Lily started to pace the floor again, pawing at the ground and reaching round to nose at her flanks as a light sweat broke out on her neck.

Georgia was beside herself. "This can't be happening, not tonight!"

Suddenly, Dan, who had been quiet until then, snapped his fingers in the air, a wide grin breaking on his face. "I've got it!" he cried as everyone turned to look at him. "It might be a bit crazy, but I think I know where we can take Lily. Dad's got a low-slung cattle trailer that has a small ramp. We're less than five minutes away and there's a clean stable waiting there that she can have her foal in. We usually use it for the orphan calves. We're on the top of the valley, so there's no danger of the yard flooding."

"I don't know," Melanie said finally. "It's just so risky, moving her. Everyone knows you shouldn't transport mares late into their pregnancies, and never so close to foaling." She had her eyes closed and was pinching her nose as she tried to take in what Dan had just proposed. It was a crazy idea, but anything had to be better than Lily foaling in the flooded yard.

Suddenly, like a miracle, the vet appeared, wading through the ankle-deep water in the yard.

"I called him, Mum," Sophie said, popping her head over the stable door.

After briefly filling the vet in on the dilemma, Georgia yelped as the water started to swirl around the door to Lily's stable. She could hear Wilson snorting next door as Callie gave another shrill cry. There was no time to lose. Dan had already phoned his dad, who was on his way with the trailer.

Nodding grimly, the vet agreed to allow Lily to be moved but only if he rode in the trailer with her.

"And me, please," Georgia said, clutching Lily's lead rope tightly. She didn't want to let her out of her sight.

"Good idea," the vet nodded. "We need to keep her as calm as possible."

Just at that moment, headlights flooded the yard, filling Georgia with relief. It was Mr Coleman in his Land Rover, towing the small cattle box behind him.

"Here, girl," he breathed as Georgia led Lily out, her legs bandaged to keep her as safe as possible for the short journey. Melanie was holding Wilson and Callie who were snorting in alarm as they high-stepped through the rising waters towards the horsebox parked up by the house.

The floodwater was nearly up to little Callie's

hocks. Her nostrils flared and she gave a shrill whinny as she fought her way out of the yard.

"Come on, darling." Georgia hugged her pony as she led her up the shallow ramp of the trailer. She thought back to when they'd had to rescue Lily from the Welsh river. Lily had instinctively known that Georgia and Dan were helping her then, just as she seemed to know it now. Looking at Georgia with huge dark eyes, Lily gently nuzzled her hand.

Chapter Twenty-Two

"How much further?" Georgia asked impatiently.

"Not long now, Georgia," said Mr Coleman. He was a steady and patient driver. Shifting slightly from side to side, Lily stood quietly as the cattle trailer rumbled down the farm lane. They were safely out of the floodwater that had engulfed the little yard at Redgrove. *Poor Melanie and Simon,* Georgia thought. She hoped they had managed to get Wilson and Callie out too, and she hoped their house was going to be OK.

As soon as the Land Rover reached the farm, Dan leapt out of the front seat and opened the door to the calves' stable. It was beautifully clean.

"Welcome to your new abode, madam." He grinned as the vet and Georgia carefully unloaded Lily.

The palomino mare gave a sigh as she walked into her stable, but it wasn't long before she began pacing again, checking her flanks.

"Got her here just in time," Mr Coleman said, leaning over the stable door. He looked completely worn out.

"In more ways than one," the vet agreed, pulling on his flat cap. "One minute longer and we would have needed a raft down at Redgrove Farm." He carefully watched the little mare, whose breath had quickened. "Easy girl, easy."

The minutes ticked by. Georgia had read in her foaling book that mares were supposed to foal within half an hour of showing signs and it had been at least twenty minutes now.

Apart from a gentle grunting sound coming from Lily, the stable was completely silent as everyone held their breath, only interrupted by the dark green lorry pulling into the yard with Wilson and Callie aboard.

Dan hurried to his feet to direct the ponies into another couple of stables before rushing back to Georgia, who was muttering under her breath, "Please Lily, please."

Her teeth were chattering, she was chilled to the bone, but that didn't matter. Nothing mattered apart from Lily and her foal. Dan put an old Barbour around her shoulders and she smiled at him gratefully. "I've rung your mum – she's on her way."

Georgia grinned at her friend. He was so thoughtful – even when his own life was being turned upside down. It would be great to have her mum there and she wanted her to share in the momentous event of Lily's foal being born.

At that moment, Lily groaned and slumped down, lying on her side, her flanks heaving.

"It's OK, it's OK," the vet said, seeing Georgia's stricken face. "This is normal. It's good. This is an early foal, but I think it's going to be OK." He pressed a finger to his lips and beckoned Georgia into the stable.

Melanie and Sophie were standing huddled outside with Dan and his dad, a mixture of concern and excitement on their faces as they watched, all silently willing for the little mare to be OK.

Squinting into the gloom, Georgia tried to make out what the vet was pointing at. Then she saw! A tiny little hoof, pointing downwards!

"A good sign," the vet smiled. "We need them pointing downwards and one slightly in front of the other."

Georgia thought her heart would crash out of her chest, it was pounding so loudly. She heard a hushed gasp come from the enchanted group of spectators outside the stable, all as enraptured as her.

"That's a girl, that's a girl," the vet was crooning, talking to Lily all the while. Her neck was now slick with sweat and her breath was coming in ragged gasps. Surely it couldn't be long now!

With one final heave and push, a small pink nose appeared, followed by the gangly, slippery body of the most perfect baby horse ever.

Georgia cried out as the foal was finally born, landing gently on the soft, pale straw.

The vet quickly set to work clearing the airways and rubbing the foal's tiny body gently, before a small kitten-like sound came from its throat.

Lily was too exhausted to move and was lying flat out with her head resting on a bank of straw. However, the little sound from her baby drove her to her feet, till she was whickering and calling for the foal.

"A colt!" the vet grinned. "And a really strong lad as well!"

Georgia looked up. There at the door beaming back at her were Dan, Mr Coleman, Melanie and Sophie – all of them reduced to tears by the birth, and, best of all, standing next to them was her mum. "I got here just in time, darling," she said. "And I'm so glad. That was the most amazing thing that I've ever seen."

Tears streamed down Georgia's cheeks as she nodded at her mum, then she turned back to watch Lily gently nudge and lick her foal dry as he tried to clamber to his feet. He was the colour of autumn leaves.

"He's so beautiful," Georgia breathed, unable to drag her eyes away from the pair.

Gently, the vet encouraged the foal to suckle, then quietly he let himself out of the stable, reassuring Georgia that she could call at any point if she was worried.

Melanie yawned. It had been a long, long day.

"Please let us stay with her," Georgia pleaded – looking from her mum to Melanie.

"Why break a habit of a lifetime?" Mrs Black smiled, referring to Lily's first night at Redgrove when Georgia had stayed with her all night following her colic. "That is – if it's OK by you, Melanie?" she asked her friend.

Melanie nodded and chuckled. "It's fine by me. But mother and baby need to have some rest now."

"The hayloft's next door," Dan said. "We could

keep an eye on them from up there, without disturbing them."

"I'd like to stay as well, Mum," said Sophie.

Melanie laughed, then she looked a bit worried again. "Guess I'll head off, then, see how Simon's getting on at home."

"I'll keep an eye on things here," Dan's father reassured the two mums, still watching the foal as he spoke and smiling for the first time in weeks.

"That would be great," said Mrs Black. "I can drive home and fetch blankets and some food."

"No need at all – we've got plenty of blankets in the house and we'll heat up some soup for everyone. Nice for me and my boys to have company tonight," Mr Coleman added a little sadly.

"Thanks so much, Mr Coleman." Georgia sighed gratefully. What would she do without all of her incredible friends?

CHAPTER TWENTY-THREE

It was almost dawn when Georgia was woken by a noise from below. She quickly glanced down into the barn.

Lily was standing quietly at the back of her stable, keeping a watchful eye on her foal. Nothing was amiss. Sophie was asleep beside her in the hay loft, curled up in a nest of blankets, her hair fanned out like a halo, the hood of her university hockey club sweater over her nose to keep off the chill and Dan was stretched out in the corner, his hands behind his head and his breathing even.

"Georgia, Georgia!" The whispering was faint but the voice was familiar.

"Emma? Is that you?" Georgia had been dozing but her senses were on full alert in case anything happened with Lily or the foal. In all of the excitement of the previous evening, Georgia had put her concerns about Emma to the back of her mind, but just before she'd drifted off to sleep she'd felt a twinge about the fact that her best friend hadn't been there for the birth of Lily's foal. And she wanted to get to the bottom of what had happened at the Show and Emma's involvement in it all. Now she sat bolt upright and peered through the darkness, hoping that it really was her friend.

It was! Emma was climbing up into the hay

hatch, and there was someone else with her. "Lexie?"

Lexie was all in black, her chestnut bob hidden beneath a dark grey beret. She was pale, her green eyes were huge in her face, and she looked as though she had been crying.

"I tried calling you, G, but I couldn't get a connection. So I rang Melanie and she told me what had happened. Georgia, please listen..." Emma's voice was urgent as she looked from Georgia to Dan, who had woken with a start and crawled over to see what was up. "Lexie's got something to tell you guys."

Lexie gave a small sob and collapsed on to the floor, waking Sophie who blinked in surprise.

Lexie was really crying now, burying her face in her hands.

"What is it?" Georgia said gently, feeling sorry for the girl.

"It's … it's…" Lexie said, unable to get her words out.

"What, Lexie?" Dan said a bit more forcibly.

She gulped and raised her eyes to look at him, the tears streaming down her cheeks.

"It's my stepdad, Joe. I've found out he's behind the farm takeover!"

✰ ✰ ✰

The small space in the loft hatch suddenly closed in on Georgia. Dan had turned white, and Sophie looked bewildered, trying to take in the news. No one spoke for what seemed like an age before Dan hissed in a quiet voice.

"What did you just say?" His hands were trembling.

"I found out just before the championships," Lexie muttered miserably. "That's why I had to get away. Joe was making me ride more and more, getting me out of the way, but not coming to shows any more. I thought he wanted me to be a showjumper like him, but then I saw a draft sale advert for River on the laptop, a few weeks ago. Then last night, while Joe was out talking to Jason, I had another look in the office to see if the advert was still there…"

Dan shook his head. "What's the sale of the pony got to do with the farm?"

"River was being sold," Lexie sobbed, looking at the ground, "to pay off some of the debts. Joe's company is in massive trouble. He needed to buy some land cheaply so he could sell it on to the supermarket in town at a profit and make money again. It was all a done deal."

"And what about the rumours that were being spread around about us?" Dan asked grimly.

Lexie nodded miserably. "It was all Delta Developments," she said, sounding distraught.

"And the break-in?" Dan had his eyes closed, as

if he couldn't quite believe what he was hearing.

Lexie started crying again. "I'd like to think Joe wasn't behind that but…" Her voice trailed off.

"Of course!" said Dan. "The 'DD' on your lorry. It stands for Delta Developments, doesn't it?"

"Yes," Lexie sniffed miserably. "Joe sits on the board. It's his company."

"And River?" Georgia said.

"All I needed to do at the Championships was jump River and win, and according to my stepdad, his price would quadruple in value," she sniffed. "I just couldn't go through with it, though – it would have meant giving him up for ever."

Emma started to speak. "Lexie didn't mean to put me in danger or mess up the team's chances," she explained. "But she knew that River wouldn't jump without her and that it would put buyers off."

"I wasn't just being selfish," said Lexie. "That's

why I had Em ride him a few times before – I thought that she might try to take my place on the team so that you could all still stand a chance in the competition and then I wouldn't have to let you all down. I can see now how stupid that was – how I could have put Emma or River in real danger. I'm an idiot, but I just didn't know what else to do."

"It's all right, Lexie," Em said, giving her friend a hug.

Georgia felt a twinge of jealousy, but then stopped herself. She had been so busy thinking about herself and her chances on the team or about Lily being pregnant that she hadn't noticed just how miserable Lexie was, nor had she realised that Emma wasn't giving up on their friendship, she was just trying to help another friend. Which was no more than Georgia would do for Dan. She hung her head. It all made sense now.

Georgia felt a pang of love for her best friend who had obviously tried to do the right thing, and all the time she'd been put out that Emma wasn't there for her at every given moment. She squeezed Emma's hand, who in turn gave her a grateful hug. There'd be plenty of time for them to talk later, but the important thing now was the future of the Colemans' farm.

"One thing I don't understand ... Seven Birches..." Georgia trailed off, not being able to put into words what she wanted to say, but Lexie seemed to understand.

"Joe always has to have the best," she said, "whether he can afford it or not." She chewed on her thumbnail. "He's overstretched himself buying that place but he was so desperate for me to follow in his riding footsteps, and to give the right impression to his clients..."

"...and you hated it," Georgia said, remembering

Lexie's white face and terrified expression at pony club.

"Yes," Lexie said, knitting her fingers together. "I hate riding in competitions and jumping. All I want to do is ride bareback and be at one with my horse."

"But you look so relaxed when you ride," said Georgia.

"Only on the flat," said Lexie. "I'm not into jumping like you…" She brushed a tear from her cheek. "All I wanted was it to be me and River, bareback riding, no competing, but my whole life Joe has pushed and pushed me."

"I hope you can forgive me for taking Em away, Georgia," she added, looking at her with huge dark eyes. "She was the only friend I ever had in my whole life. I've never had the kind of friendship the two of you have."

Georgia smiled kindly at Lexie. How wrong she

194

had been – thinking that Lexie had everything that she could wish for and more. Georgia and her mum may not be rich and Lily may only be on loan to her, but she had never felt luckier in her whole life!

"OK!" Dan clapped his hands, snapping her out of her thoughts and making them both jump. "That's enough about that. We'll sort out River for you later, Lexie," he promised her. "But first … we need to save the farm!"

Emma looked a little shy. "Actually, you don't need to worry about that," she said. "Dad's on to it," she said mysteriously. "Lexie and I have been with him tonight. He's got together the proof that the burglary and the rumours were deliberate to make your dad sell the farm. He's coming over first thing in the morning to stop the takeover!"

"Really?" Dan's eyes widened. "I can't believe it! I have to go and tell Dad!"

✩ ✪ ✩

There didn't seem much point in trying to go back to sleep now. Instead, Emma and Georgia grabbed a moment to creep down to see Lily while Sophie looked after Lexie. Dan had hurtled out of the hay barn to go and share the news with his dad and brother.

The perfect little colt twitched and stirred as he slept soundly at Lily's hooves. Although she was alert, clearly protecting her newborn, the palomino's cream-coloured tail swished contentedly as she stood over her foal.

"He's amazing," Emma breathed.

"Isn't he?" Georgia replied. She didn't think she had ever seen such a precious thing. Lily looked up and whickered very quietly at Georgia in greeting.

Emma tucked her arm through her friend's. "I wish I had been here for the birth."

"I've missed you so much," Georgia said to her.

"I know, and I'm so sorry." Emma looked upset. "I was jealous that you got all the attention at Redgrove, but I should have talked to you about it." She looked ashamed. "At first, it felt really good to be riding at Seven Birches. I missed you too, but I felt I had to stay for Lexie – she was so unhappy but she wouldn't tell me why, and I thought she was going to do something stupid, like…"

"Run away?" Georgia said.

"Yeah," Emma smiled. "And I guess I know why now."

CHAPTER TWENTY-FOUR

It was still only first light when the two girls made their way up the drive to the Colemans' farm. Dan and his father and brother stood in a huddle, deep in conversation. Georgia guessed that Dan had caught up with them while they were doing their routine dawn round of all of the animals. They looked as though they hadn't slept much, but there was something much more positive about

Mr Coleman's stance, like the weight of the world was beginning to lift off his shoulders.

"Morning, girls," Mr Coleman greeted them. "We were just on our way inside. The agents from Delta Developments will be here any moment. We were due to sign the deal first thing this morning."

While Mr Coleman made a pot of tea, he asked Emma to go over the details of what she and Lexie had found out.

"So, let's get this straight," said Dan's dad. "Lexie's father owns Delta Developments and at the same time as take over the farm, they were also trying to discredit us?"

"Exactly," replied Georgia. "After you said you weren't interest in selling, they had to find a way to force your hand."

"Apparently Joe only intended to hold on to the land for a matter of days before he sold it on," Emma explained.

"It's a lot to take in." Mr Coleman sighed heavily as he brought the teapot over to the kitchen table. "The trouble is, the bank's never going to let me keep the farm now. I still have to sell, otherwise we have no means of paying all the bills."

"Not so." A face appeared around the kitchen door.

"Dad!" Emma jumped up.

"Hi, darling," he grinned, putting his briefcase on the table. He was dressed smartly in a pinstriped suit and a red tie and looked as though he meant business. "I've been looking into the company's dealings," he said, launching straight into an explanation for Mr Coleman. "As you heard, Lexie came to see me yesterday. She got a taxi all the way to our house when she was supposed to be jumping. It didn't take me long to verify what she told me." He looked a little crestfallen for a second. 'I'm very disappointed that someone who has been a long-term business associate and friend of mine could operate so dishonestly, but he has. I've got the proof and, with your permission, Mr Coleman, I should be able to help you out of this sticky situation."

Dan's father was about to speak when there was a commotion out in the yard. A black saloon had pulled up, scattering the chickens and sending Hattie into a frenzy of barking. It was the agents. Quickly, Emma's dad tapped a number into his mobile and, excusing himself, went into the hallway and started talking in hushed tones.

The two visitors knocked on the kitchen door, and without waiting for it to be opened, brazenly let themselves in.

Extending a hand towards Dan's father, one of the men spoke. "So, Mr Coleman, I hope you're ready to sign the papers?"

Dan's father declined the handshake and shook his head. Calmly he got to his feet and in a level but firm voice said, "Gentleman, I would like to show you the door. There will be no deal today." The agents both looked indignant and one opened his mouth to object. Mr Coleman waved him away as Emma's dad re-entered the room. "Or if you're intent on staying, perhaps you might be interested in what my friend here has to say." He gestured towards Emma's dad who had removed a small black file from his briefcase.

For the first time, Georgia saw the arrogant looks on the agents' faces turn to ones of uncertainty.

Emma's father smiled a cool, hard smile. "I think the police might be interested in the contents of this, don't you?" he said, opening the file. "False rumours started to keep buyers away, a break-in, oh, and not to mention the current financial situation of the company and your deal with the supermarket."

Speechless, and looking increasingly awkward, the two men started to back away towards the kitchen door, gathering up their briefcases as they went.

"Please don't hurry, gentlemen," Mr Clark added, as a police car drove slowly up the drive, blocking in the black saloon's exit. "I think someone wants a word with you…"

✩ ✪ ✩

"High five, Dad!" Emma whooped once the police had escorted the agents off the premises with the promise that Delta Development's dealings were going to be fully investigated, and Mr Coleman wasn't going to lose the farm.

Lexie and Sophie had come up to the farmhouse together just in time to hear the good news, and Dan and Ben were hugging everyone. There was a real celebratory mood in the kitchen and only Lexie remained quiet, huddled in the corner with her arms around Hattie. Georgia went to sit down beside her.

"What you did was really brave, you know," she said gently.

"Not brave," Lexie shook her head. "Just the right thing. I don't know how Mum's going to take it, that's all," she said. "She's used to the high life and there's no doubt about it – it's going to be downhill from now on."

"It will all work out," Georgia said, hugging her. "Things always do when you do the right thing."

Lexie bit her bottom lip and buried her face in Hattie's fur. "All I really care about is being able to keep River, but I think I'm going to lose him as well..."

✩ ✪ ✩

As with most villages, it didn't take long for the

news to spread like wildfire – not only about the saving of the farm but of the dramatic rescue of Lily and her unborn foal too. By mid-morning a few curious customers were pulling up the drive to the Colemans' Farm to take a look and see the miracle foal and Lily. Ben was soon opening up the shop and dishing out hot soup. Melanie and Simon were among the visitors, coming over to check on Lily and her foal as well as Callie and Wilson.

"Sorry we weren't here a bit earlier," Melanie said, looking Lily over. "The water didn't reach the house, thank goodness, and it's subsided now, but the yard's in a bit of a mess." She smiled, looking tired.

Simon reached a hand out to the little colt. "But at least we got all the horses out just in time and we're fully insured."

"That's good news," Georgia said. Then she

spontaneously hugged Melanie. "I'm so happy for Lily! We watched her nearly all night. She's the best mum in the world!"

Simon beamed.

"She couldn't ask for someone better to look after her than you, Georgia," Melanie told her, tousling her hair.

Georgia blushed with pleasure as Dan came over to join them.

"If your dad's OK with it, Dan, we'll move her back in a few days when the foal's a little stronger," Simon said.

"I'm sure that will be just fine." Dan grinned. "Lily's welcome here and there are lots of people eager to meet her!"

At that moment a small girl tugged on Georgia's arm and gazed up at her. "Are you Lily's owner?" she asked, grinning a gappy grin.

"Sort of!" Georgia laughed.

"Then please can I have your autograph?"

The girl's mum smiled. "As soon as she heard about the foal being born in the floods she wanted to come straight over here," she explained.

"See!" Dan said laughing loudly. "Lily's going to bring the business back!"

"She's the best," Georgia smiled. "The very best…"

CHAPTER TWENTY-FIVE

After that the days flew by in a whirl. There must have been at least a hundred people who came to the farm to see Lily and her foal. Ben and Dan were in their element serving all of their returning customers. The farm shop had never been busier – especially as the news spread about the failed takeover. There were still bills to be paid, of course, but the bank had given them an extension on a loan and it looked like things were going to work out.

One evening, when all the ponies had been moved back to Redgrove and Lily had settled her foal into his new home, Georgia slipped into the stable to see how they were getting on. She placed her arms around the little palomino and Lily whickered with pleasure. Even the foal nuzzled her, before skipping around excitedly once more.

Dan, who had come to visit, had just turned Wilson and Callie out into the small paddock next to the yard. Neither of the ponies strayed far from the fence, their eyes never leaving Lily's stable door as they kept an eye on their friend.

"Hey, clever girl," Georgia whispered and Lily sighed in contentment.

Just then, Dan leaned in over the stable door and chuckled as the foal nudged his hand, wiggling his fluffy tail. "He really is perfect," he said.

Georgia smiled, sitting down on the straw next to Lily as Dan let himself in and settled down beside her.

"I still can't believe we get to stay at the farm," he said, shaking his head.

"I know." Georgia grinned. "It's amazing."

"Does this one have a name yet?" Dan stroked the foal's nose as the little pony curiously sniffed the welly boots Dan was wearing, before skipping back to the safety of Lily who nudged him gently.

"His name is Secret," Georgia said proudly. "I thought it was appropriate, somehow, with everything that's gone on. I told Eric that was what he was called when I sent him those photos, and he thinks it's a great name."

"It *is* a great name," Dan agreed and together they sat, watching Lily and the newly christened Secret until the sun set once again on Redgrove Farm, and another day.

✰ ✰ ✰

"I hope she's going to be OK," Georgia said, talking about Lexie as she and Emma hacked down the country lane the following weekend. The Haydens had cleared up the yard and, despite there still being some flood damage to sort out, true to her word, Melanie had organised a loan pony for Emma to ride – it was a cob gelding that needed exercising regularly.

Lexie hadn't appeared at school on the Monday following the flood weekend or for the rest of that week. Nor had Emma been able to get hold of her.

"So do I," said Emma. "She'll contact me when she can."

Word had spread that Joe was facing a hefty fine for failing to stop the actions of the board, possibly even a jail sentence, and that his company was facing financial ruin. A "For Sale" sign hung outside the gated entrance to Seven Birches, and the yard looked deserted and empty.

"It's good news about the Colemans' farm," commented Emma.

"It sure is," replied Georgia.

The local newspaper had been full of the story all week, and this time Dan had been proud to see the headline on the stand in the little newsagents. Mr Coleman had never had so many letters or cards, all full of support for his farm business.

As Emma and Georgia headed up to Redgrove Farm together, the ponies' hooves kicked through the piles of fallen leaves that carpeted the drive up to the yard.

They turned the corner to find a surprise there ahead of them. Sitting on the stonewall, a familiar figure gave them a little wave. There was a small horsebox parked in the drive with the words "EB Horse Transport" emblazoned on the side, and a woman with blonde hair sitting in the driver's seat.

"Lexie?" Emma gasped and rushed forward to hug her old friend.

Lexie was wearing jeans and an old hoody and looked like a normal teenager rather than someone on their way to the Horse of the Year Show as she normally did.

"Hey," she said, smiling at them both. "I've come to say goodbye." She gestured at the horsebox and her mum, before opening the side door.

An appaloosa pony, bandaged up and wearing a dark green rug, surveyed them calmly, munching on a hay net.

"River!" Georgia gasped. "You're keeping him!"

"Yes, I am," Lexie said proudly. "Once Mum found out about Joe and his debts, that was it. It's been over for a long time between them, actually. Once Mum and I had a really good talk about everything she decided to take over ownership of

River. But we've lost everything else." Her eyes clouded over. "Herbie's been sold and the others, but Janey helped us find really good homes for them." She traced her shoe around in the dust. "Joe wasn't all bad, you know," she said. "Deep down he was a good person but things spiralled out of control and he always wanted more. I hope he's going to be OK."

There was a moment's silence between the three girls and then Emma broke it by asking, "Where are you going now?" She had noticed the suitcases piled up in the living compartment of the horsebox.

"Back to Yorkshire," Lexie said. "Staying with Mum's parents in their cottage till we find our feet. River's staying at a DIY livery yard that sounds really nice. I can practise my natural horsemanship and I don't ever have to jump again." Lexie smiled a small sad smile before hugging them both tightly. "Keep in touch, won't you?" she said, as she

climbed into the horsebox next to her mum, who
gave them a little wave as she started the engine.

☆ ✧ ☆

"It's funny, isn't it?" Emma mused later as they
tidied the yard for the evening, sweeping the last
few shavings off the cobbles. She leaned on her
broom and gazed at the ponies in their stables –
Wilson in his hood, Callie with a fluffy winter coat,
and Lily and her foal both wearing navy rugs.
They were peacefully finishing up their suppers
and had full hay nets waiting. Secret was suckling
from his mother, his eyes closed. He had already
grown loads! "I mean, how someone can have so
much, but so little really…"

Georgia nodded, understanding immediately
and remembering her own thoughts about Lexie
on the night that Secret had been born.

She gave her best friend a hug. It was so brilliant
to have Emma back on the yard regularly and to

be able to share everything with her again.

At that moment, Dan came strolling through the gates, a huge grin on his face. He was always in an extremely good mood these days.

As it was a Friday night they were going to go to the cinema together and then for pizza afterwards, and Georgia couldn't wait to spend some time with her two best friends.

"Come on, Georgia!" Emma said, stowing the yard brush. "Your mum will be here in a minute to give us a lift."

"I'll meet you out front in a sec," Georgia said. "I just want to say good night to Lily and Secret."

"No change there then," Emma laughed, pretending to roll her eyes. "Race you to the gate, Dan!"

And the two of them were off, their laughter filling the air.

Georgia let herself into Lily's stable and hugged

her pony. Secret bounded over and nudged her hand playfully. Georgia could hardly believe he could stay upright on his skinny little legs but he seemed so full of energy!

The palomino snuffled her gently, breathing sweet, warm pony breath into her hair.

"Thank you, Lily, for everything," she whispered. "Eric was right. You *did* come into my life for a reason … a very special reason… And like he said, no matter what happens, however bad it seems, somehow, you always help me find my way through."

ACKNOWLEDGEMENTS

Nosy Crow would like to thank Katy Marriott Payne for letting her lovely Palomino pony star on the covers of this series.